My Last Confession

My Last Confession

Helen FitzGerald

faber and faber

First published in 2009
by Faber and Faber Limited
3 Queen Square London WC1N 3AU

Photoset by
Printed in England by

A CIP record for this book
is available from the British Library

ISBN 978-0-571-23967-2

2 4 6 8 10 9 7 5 3 1

ONE

Tips for Parole Officers:
1. Don't smuggle heroin into prison.
2. Don't drink vodka to relieve stress.
3. Don't French-kiss a colleague to get your boyfriend jealous.
4. Don't snort speed.
5. Don't spend more time with murderers than with your son.
6. Don't invite crack-head clients to your party.

Maybe if they'd had some kind of induction then my wedding day would have been the most wonderful day of my life. I would have beamed in my mermaid sheath with floral-embroidered bust. Robbie would have walked in front of me in his Hunting Donald kilt, mini sporran, maxi smile, his hair lacquered, fifties-style, his battery-operated diesel engine whirring in his shirt pocket. He might have thrown rose petals on our friends and families and said 'shite' very loudly as I had accidentally taught him to do. And Chas would have lifted the veil from my face and kissed me on the lips, making me the happiest bride in the history of brides.

I should have watched dewy-eyed as Chas made a toast to us and a speech. Instead, someone pinned me down and I clawed at the dark like Clarice Starling.

I should have waltzed with Chas. Instead, I had to watch his life slipping away while I screamed for someone to call an ambulance, please . . . *please* . . .

I

I should have sipped champagne. Instead I sobbed with terror.

It was all my fault. Because in my first month in the job I was stupid enough to do all those things a parole officer should never do.

In the two years before I became a parole officer I'd made a lot of changes in my life. I'd given up work to concentrate on bringing up my baby, Robbie. I'd watched him learn how to crawl then walk then talk then body-slam my boyfriend Chas till the two of them were sore with laughter. Most of all, I had dived headfirst into the realm of the loved.

I let myself drink a cup of coffee in bed each morning while Chas went back to sleep beside me. I enjoyed the time we spent holding the buggy handles together as we mooched around not-very-good shops. I took turns with Chas in pushing the swing at the park, making funny shapes with bubbles in the bath, reading stories, lying beside Robbie till he fell asleep.

And Chas and I touched. In fact we never stopped touching. I just couldn't get enough of this person I'd held at a distance for so many years.

To start with, the three of us lived off the goodwill of my parents. In my hour of need one sunny September they emptied the essentials from my flat into their house and fluffed themselves up around me for as long as I needed. They encouraged routine, good food, exercise and fresh air. They discouraged drinking, impulsiveness, self-hate and blame. My routine became the same as Robbie's. After a good night's sleep, I ate the spoonfuls of sustenance that Mum and Dad set before me. Mid morning, I took slow, calm walks around the park. I slurped home-made soup for lunch, snoozed in the afternoon, went for a second stroll in the evening, ate a balanced dinner, had a bath some time later and then went to bed. It bored me stupid to start with. No alcohol, no partying, no friends, colleagues, worries and buzzes. Just the calming presence of Chas and my parents. But before long I began to redefine what I previously called boredom as relaxation and good health and realised that these things were gradually leading me towards happiness.

Chas started off by visiting, then staying over occasionally. He'd been released from prison a couple of years back, after assaulting a paedophile, who just happened to be the step-father of my closest childhood friend, Sarah. For years this man had set about ruining the lives of children he had unsu-pervised access to. He'd almost ruined mine, and had suc-ceeded spectacularly with Sarah. It was terrible in my eyes that Chas had been punished so severely.

After his release, Chas was paroled to his family home in Edinburgh. His parents were posh serious types who wanted Chas to turn his life around, get a sensible job and a differ-ent girlfriend. Ever the rebel, he continued to paint and com-muted to my house as often as he could.

When Chas declared that he was no longer on parole and could therefore live wherever he wanted, I asked him to move in. He kissed his worried parents goodbye and arrived at the door with two large suitcases. Each morning after that, Chas would head off to the space he'd rented at the sculp-ture studios in Hillfoot and spend his day painting from the sketches he'd made all over the world. He'd travelled for years after we shared a flat at Uni, sketching his way through latitudes, but after he came back, and we got together, he hid them from me. It was a surprise, he said. He'd show me if he ever had an exhibition.

It took time, but I was gradually coming to terms with the death of my best friend, Sarah. Her name always followed the word 'poor' in my mind. Poor Sarah had a terrible child-hood. Poor Sarah couldn't get pregnant. Poor Sarah was betrayed by her husband, Kyle, and her best friend – me.

Poor Sarah killed herself.

After months of waking to a sick feeling in my tummy, with poor Sarah's face hovering over my bed, I began to feel better. I felt like I had everything a girl could possibly hope for:

A beautiful healthy three-year-old son who made up songs to the tune of the Teletubbies:

> *Mum and Daddy*
> *Mum and Daddy*
> *Eat fried rice*
> *Mum and Daddy*
> *Mum and Daddy*
> *Are ve . . . ry nice!*
> *(And I saw them kissing . . . YUK!)*

A loving partner who always had the time and energy to hold and comfort me; who knew how to change my negative thoughts to positive ones, my bad moods to good; who always had the right answer when I asked him, sometimes in the middle of the night, if everything was going to be okay. 'Yes, baby girl,' he would reply. 'Everything is perfect, because I love you more than anything in the world. I even love you more than pizza.'

(Chas really loved pizza.)

I had two wonderful, generous parents who had put weekend getaways on hold and given over two of their precious bedrooms to help get me back on track.

And I had an immensely good haircut. After wearing it long and wavy for years, and mostly shoving it back in a ponytail to get it out of the way, one day when a wonderful feeling overtook the sickly one in my tummy, I decided it was time for layers. I called Jenny, hairdresser to the stars and me, and she layered it with glee till I looked glowingly thirty-five, and for days afterwards everyone stopped me to say how terrific I looked.

The haircut signalled the end of a phase in my life and the beginning of another. It was time to move back into my own flat, time to get a job. I was ready to get back out there, into the real world.

I think Mum and Dad were ready too. Mum missed her creative room, which had been taken over by wooden train tracks and a cot-bed, and Dad missed the spare bedroom Chas and I slept in, which he had used to decamp to when Mum got fidgety feet in the middle of the night.

I gave my tenants a month's notice and we started packing up our gear and organising to get stuff out of storage.

With Chas no longer on parole, I decided to apply for a position in criminal justice. The job was very different from the child protection work I'd done for so long and that had helped burn me to a cinder two years earlier – safer, somehow, because I would be following the orders of the court. I wouldn't be taking people's children away from them or accusing them of things. No, I would be part of the criminal justice system and therefore secure in the knowledge that my clients would not blame me, harm me or hate my guts. Also, a friend of mine had worked with offenders and said it was way more family-friendly than child protection. And I have to admit that the idea of talking to bad boys all day seemed as exciting as when I was a teenager.

One night after Robbie went to sleep, I filled out an application form for 'Criminal Justice Social Worker'. I wrote a beautiful covering letter about being a team player, understanding the balance between care and control, having outstanding time-management skills and all the other crap they wanted to hear.

I posted it the next day.

TWO

When I got dressed on the morning of the interview, guilt, self-hate and nerves competed for the space in my head where my brain used to be. Was my decision to go back to work the right one? Or was Zach's mum's choice a better one? Play-group treasurer? Taxi service for promising young swimmer, gymnast, baby-yoga-ist, sing-alonger and enjoy-a-baller? Maker of time-tabled, organic, E-numberless and aggressively supervised meals? Mother of children who knew their place, their manners, their alphabets and their keyboards? Campaigner against the word 'just' as a prefix for housewife?

Or was Martha's mum right? Casual dope smoker who laughed with her little one, enjoyed every moment she spent with her, even if she sometimes forgot to make dinner as such. Then again, as Martha's mum reasoned, if the wee one was really hungry then she'd ask for food, wouldn't she?

Or was it me? Rummaging through my clothes saying fuck and shite a lot, sculling a tepid Lavazza, getting ready to leave Robbie behind in his warm Bob the Builder PJs?

Of all three mums, as I got dressed for my interview that morning, I knew I was the *least* right.

Expletives done for the moment, I dragged an old social work uniform out of my cupboard – not too 'I'm-superior-to-you' formal, not too 'I-can-be-walked-all-over' casual – and kissed my boys goodbye.

If I got the job, Chas planned to take the Robster to the studio with him. 'Don't be so traditional, K!' he said. 'You're so het up. He'll be fine!' Robbie would be given a paint brush

6

and some old canvases and it would be fun, Chas insisted – two boys with paint, hanging out – what could possibly go wrong?

(Ha! I was looking forward to Chas clambering up that learning curve.)

Chas and Robbie waved from the front door of Mum and Dad's, both beaming at me as I walked along the street and turned the corner. As I disappeared, I heard in the distance that Robbie's giggling had turned to crying, and it was like when I was breastfeeding and milk would spurt from my breasts when Robbie cried, which was horrifying, but also wonderful, how the connection between us was so physical. We were joined then, and still were because although milk wasn't spurting from my tits (thank goodness, as I had a lovely black shirt on) his cry went to a place in me that no other cry ever could. I ran back to him, but by the time I got there Chas had distracted him by tickling him under the chin with a Chinese lantern from the neighbour's garden. Looking up at me from his laughing, it was clear he was wondering why the hell I was back so soon. So I tickled him too, and kissed Chas on his beautiful perfect painter's hands, the hands I'd fallen in love with two years earlier in the backseat of a Ford. Then I turned and ran all the way to my car with a different kind of pain, the kind that's more like an ache because at the end of the day, even as a mother, you're not indispensable.

It pissed with rain as I walked past two high-rise towers plonked in the middle of a wasteland. Wind channelled its way between them, the towers swaying. I looked up and wondered about who was swaying up there, twenty-two storeys high, their stained tea mugs sliding left then right on their kitchen tables. It made me dizzy, so I looked down and concentrated on walking, which wasn't easy because the wind was pushing me as if to say, *Get out of here, out of here.*

7

The interview was at my prospective workplace, which was in an area of deprivation. If only I'd heeded the warning – i.e. an area that is the puddle of the world; an area with boarded-up windows and unplayed-in playgrounds; an area with more wind than other areas just yards away, more wind and no street names, no house numbers and no pedestrian crossings; an area not to be entered lightly, but with a knife and a willingness to use it. People walked on the road, refusing to defer to the moneyed authority of cars. Groups of young men stood on corners dealing, or else eating Gregg's steak bites.

I walked past them, wondering if they would notice that an outsider was walking by. Someone from a different place, only two miles away, but a place with house numbers, Lavazza and hope.

The interview went badly. Suddenly I wanted to be home with Robbie more than anything in the world, especially considering the dire state of the office and surrounds. Still, I tried my best to feign enthusiasm as I sat on my rickety chair in the middle of a large ugly room filled with shite and three interviewers.

In the social work course I did there'd been many important things to learn – risk assessment, anti-discrimination, crisis intervention and so on. But one of the most important lessons, the thing that everyone who did the course learned by heart and kept with them for life, was to dress so appallingly that the users at the meth clinic felt chic in comparison.

These three had pushed the lesson a bit too far, however. Take the style and elegance of committed Christians, quadruple it, and you have the three social workers who interviewed me that day. Commendable, determined ugliness, taken to the limit, from tip to toe, in greasy hair, bad teeth, and clothing too small or too large but worth it for the price.

As they sat opposite me, bombarding me with questions, I remembered why I'd felt so good when I left social work. Social workers were intensely serious and quite often they had bad breath.

I had done the wrong course, was going for the wrong job, I thought to myself as I licked the back of my hand and smelt it.

(Oh . . . coffee tongue. Maybe not.)

The questions were the same as for my first interview ten years earlier, and I answered them half-heartedly, rambling on about the things I remembered from the relevant sections of my diploma. I made an attempt at humour: 'My weaknesses?' I repeated. 'Well, there's my perfectionism, which can be a bit difficult, and I'm a workaholic, can't get enough of work, you know . . . which can also be a bit hard. And then there's my cocaine habit . . .'

My boss-to-be, an expressionless forty-something with a voice so soft and therapeutic that I wanted to strangle her, did not flinch. The two men bookending her bit their lips, bless them.

I left the grey building thanking the lord that I'd fucked it up so badly. Who'd work in a place like *that*? Where would you go for lunch?

But when I got home they'd already phoned with the good news. I was now a criminal justice social worker or, in sexier terms, a probation officer, parole officer, shit-kicking, hard-talking, bad-boy-breaching administrator of the law. If it'd been America, I'd have had a gun and a uniform – that's how Goddam sexy my new job was.

The next day, Chas bought me a police uniform and a toy gun, and he was mightily pleased, if a little sore, at how quickly and naturally my shit-kicking-bad-boy-breaching attitude had taken hold.

9

THREE

Mum and Dad were happy for us. We were starting a new life together, like they had, thirty-seven years earlier. A couple of nights before we moved out, we found ourselves all sitting around looking at their wedding photos. They got married in Bali, long before it was fashionable and the likes of Mick Jagger and Jerry Hall tied the knot – or not – there. Afterwards, they partied with four friends till the wee hours before falling asleep on the beach.

'We were so in love!' Mum said, smiling, because they still were, after thirty-seven years together. They still sought each other out at parties ahead of anyone else, still had stuff to say over formal restaurant tables.

'Chas is a lucky boy,' Mum told me, and we hugged.

'I don't deserve him,' I said. At this she pushed my fringe back, oddly fond of my forehead and eyebrows, and told me that I had no self-awareness, and that everyone was always inordinately pleased to see me. She told me that, at Christmas time, aunts and uncles and cousins would sit at the table not saying much until I arrived and then conversation would suddenly start. I brought laughter to people, she continued. Did I not realise that Chas was flat as a pancake without me? Withdrawn and sad.

'Try and be a bit more sensible!' she said. 'But never lose that light you have, and believe me, you deserve him.'

I went to bed loving myself, but also realising that my mum and dad just knew how to breed happiness. In everything they did and said, they bred happiness, and this was my lucky inheritance.

It was raining by the time we finished packing the car with all our stuff. I hugged Mum then Dad and we all had tears in our eyes. We drove with the wipers on all the way over to the West End, and had to park an impossible distance from my flat. And even though the parking was a pain, it was great to be back where residents varied in colour and style. I bounced up the close with Chas and Robbie, desperate for my bath, my spices, our home.

We spent the first day toddler-proofing cupboards and windows and loos and following the Robster around as he found other things that needed to be toddler-proofed.

That night I put him to bed and walked into the kitchen to find Chas with chilled champagne and a beautifully wrapped present.

'To our new life together!' he said, popping the cork and pouring the fizz.

I took a sip and opened the present, with the gooey, lovey-dovey expectation of a newly-wed. The paper was pink and shiny, and so was the rabbit vibrator inside.

'Chas!' I said, beholding the rubber-eared cock.

'Guaranteed orgasm!' he said.

Oh God, not this again.

I'd never had one. An orgasm that is. Despite twenty-two sexual partners (or twenty-three, depending on your definition), I'd never had one. I'd never even admitted to not having one, not till the first time I slept with Chas.

We were at Mum and Dad's house, in the den at the time. Robbie was asleep in the creative room, and Mum and Dad were watching television. Chas had been very patient with me, but as much as he treasured having his hands caressed, he was horny as a bastard and no amount of finger sucking in conjunction with pud-pulling would satisfy him.

We'd just cuddled etcetera etcetera for nights on end, but this time I knew I was ready and when we finished I sighed happily because it was the best sex I'd ever had.

'That was the best sex I've ever had,' I said.

'Really?' he asked.

'Yes,' I was defensive now. 'Why?'

'It's just that you didn't . . .' he said.

'What?'

'You didn't, you know, climax.'

'Yes I did.'

'Krissie . . .'

'I did!' I shouted, getting out of bed in a strop and going to the bathroom. How dare he accuse me of not coming? Of course I had. I was thirty-five and I'd never come so completely for over two decades!

He was behind me in the bathroom, sheepish. I washed my hands and tried to walk out of the bathroom, but he barricaded the door with his arms. There was a struggle. Me trying to get out from under one arm, the other, under his legs, and so on, to no avail.

I ended up on the floor and crying. 'I don't think I ever have,' I said, my face in my hands, embarrassed.

I wasn't sure in the same way I wasn't sure if I'd been in love before I undoubtedly fell into it with Chas. There'd been times when I missed a man so much I ached. Could have been love. Times when I didn't eat for days after it ended. Possibly. Likewise I'd had sexual experiences that made me smile for days, ones that made me cry, and certainly I'd regularly made loud animal noises. But Chas spotted a mile away that my noises were never loud nor animal enough to suggest the oblivion of a werewolf-like transformation. And this was what I should aim for, he explained: oblivion – eyes white and flickering, mouth stretched and uneven with all the distortions and discomfort of a human possessed.

Sounded bloody awful, I'd reckoned, but Chas was always right, always knew best. So that's why I didn't mind when he bought me the rabbit that Saturday, the special gel on Sunday, the vibrating eggs on Monday, a lacy Anne Summers number four nights in a row and sporadic buzzers for the following two weeks. We were on a mission to find me an orgasm.

Initially, we placed the rabbit on the coffee table well after Robbie's bedtime, to get accustomed to it. In truth, I found the huge rubber penis-shaped object quite frightening, but it remained on the coffee table for at least two Big Brother evictions, oft-times buzzing towards us like a Dalek. So I was no longer frightened of it by the time Chas moved the bunny and his entourage into the bedroom.

He devised other exercises: just touching each other with no penetrative sex for five days; female-perspective porn that didn't involve harsh nipple-twisting and too much pink thrust; shower attachments and lengthy periods alone 'just to learn'.

I'd love to say I didn't need my rubber friend in the end; that all I needed was a new, blank mind and the love and patience of a man who smelt of everything good in the world – toast, cut grass, the smoke of a roaring campfire. But I can't say that, because Chas was out painting in his studio, and I was alone and pressing hard on my bunny's ears when I suddenly found myself to be the scariest, ugliest werewolf on the moors.

I was thirty-five, and I knew, at last.

FOUR

A few days later, Chas and Robbie got ready for their first day together at the sculpture studio. There were many things Robbie needed to be official Painter's Assistant. Paintbrush? Tick. Huge old T-shirt? Tick. Ridiculously large beret? Tick. By the time Robbie was 'dressed for work', his teeny chin and his wee white neck were the only bits of him that were actually visible. After kissing and giggling at the front door, we parted ways. Before I headed down to my car, I watched them walking up Gardner Street hand in hand, blissfully happy.

It took me twenty-five minutes to drive to work, then another twenty-five to park. The car park was packed with the cheap cars of council employees. The building was an old textiles factory that architects had somehow managed to convert into something even more depressing.

I found my way to the reception area, and stood at the bench wondering how to achieve eye contact with the person whose nose was ten inches from mine. A cough? A finger-nail-tap on the bench? Words?

'Hi, I'm Krissie Donald,' I said, expecting this information to be enough to initiate action. It didn't even initiate eye contact.

'In Hilary Sweeney's team,' I said. 'Criminal justice.'

'No one told us,' said the lucky-result-of-a-policy-to-employ-locals.

After I fake-smiled, she begrudgingly opened the trapdoor that separated agitated clients from agitated typists, and led me through the messy admin area, out the back and up two floors, to a small office crammed with four desks.

'There, have that one,' she said, then left.

I sat at the empty desk for half an hour before three people filtered in.

'Fuck me!' said the first. 'They've finally filled it then!' He was forty-five, six foot six and – I soon learnt – had three degrees and did stand-up comedy in his spare time, most of which appeared to be in the office.

'I'm Robert,' he added, before telling me a joke that answered any questions about the level of political correctness in my workplace (low).

'Are you crazy? Must be fucking crazy to be in this place,' said the second, Danny, a gorgeous-looking guy with shaded glasses and very shiny shoes. 'Like your top, by the way,' he said, sitting down at a desk opposite me and turning on his computer.

'Thanks,' I said.

The computer started speaking to him and he pulled out a tampon-shaped object and began sucking on it. 'Windows on,' said the computer. 'Outlook. Open . . . Inbox . . . You have five new messages . . .'

'Is it new?' he asked me.

'Sorry?' I said. The talking computer had made me forget the topic of our small talk.

'Your top?'

'No,' I replied, while six-foot-six Robert made a Shhh gesture at me, then snuck around behind Danny to place a device under the receiver of his phone. Unaware, Danny sucked his nicotine inhaler again, then picked up the phone, which exploded so loudly that I felt immediate gratitude for whoever invented panty liners.

There was a moment's silence, and then Danny grabbed a stick from under his desk and whisked it around behind him till it smashed Robert in the knees.

That's when I realised that Danny was completely blind.

After that, I could hardly take my eyes off him. The way he typed, read Braille, put numbers into his wee electronic talking book, answered the phone and talked.

'He's too sick to come in, is he, Mrs Thom?' he said to the mother of the 9 a.m. non-show. 'So is he dying? Bleeding? Has his voice box been shot?' (A muffled response.) 'No? In that case put him on.' (More muffle.) 'Well get him out of bed!'

Danny waited.

'Peter. Last week I gave you a second formal warning for being aggressive and racist in reception . . .'

Another interval.

'PETER! It's irrelevant whether or not asylum seekers are using up all your social workers. The point is you're breached, mate. You're going back in.'

With this, my new blind hero hung up his phone, sucked once more on his nicotine inhaler and continued our conversation.

'It's nice, the top, but it doesn't go with those trousers.'

My third colleague was large, serious and over fifty, with an accent that smacked of 'doing the job for charity'. Her name was Penny and she was immensely active with her paperwork, her face red and sweaty with the effort of it.

The boss, Hilary, was one of the three who had interviewed me. While her male seniors at least had smiles to suppress as I'd made inappropriate quips, she'd had no such problem. Smiles were for clients only and did not indicate joviality.

After a reasonably relaxed morning with my three colleagues, Hilary sat me down in her office, which was directly opposite ours, for my first supervision session, much of which centred around diarising future supervision sessions. With twelve fortnightly meet-ups inked, Hilary then talked for an hour without pausing, enjoying the sound of her own voice so much her mouth frothed with the pleasure of it.

'Transparency is essential', she said, 'to our robust packages of care, which combine effective monitoring and a therapeutic approach that addresses and ameliorates the issues surrounding the risk of recidivism.'

I nodded at appropriate intervals, trying hard to understand what the hell she was talking about, and praised the Lord when she handed me two report requests and let me loose.

Back in the office, Robert was pinning chocolate wrappers to Danny's 'Wall of Shame' and Penny was banging heavy wads of her paper around her desk and huffing.

I sat down at my jiggly desk and looked at the first report request, a home background report for Jason Marney. A sticky note on top said: 'Overdue! Case Conf, Sandhill, 4 p.m.' Jason Marney was a widower of thirty-nine, and had spent twelve months behind bars for lewd and libidinous practices against his children. Fuck, a sex offender. I'd hoped to avoid those guys. He had four offences – two indecent exposures ten and eight years back respectively, one indecent assault at a swimming pool two years ago, and the lewd and lib. According to the indictment, he'd made his four- and six-year-old boys watch hardcore porn with him and got them to take turns touching his genitals. Blah. Serious, big-time stomach-churning blah. Still, I consoled myself, the report was a basic one. Mr Marney wanted to be released to his parents' address in Toryglen. All I had to do was check that the accommodation was safe and suitable, and then beg Hilary not to allocate me as his supervising officer after his release. It'd be a push, but I could visit his parents before the 4 p.m. case conference.

The second report request was a pre-trial report for Jeremy Bagshaw.

I didn't realise it at the time, but it was this case that would almost ruin my life.

FIVE

Jeremy Bagshaw had spent most of the previous two weeks trying not to cry. It wasn't okay to cry in Sandhill. In fact, it was the opposite of okay. Tough guys going for you, officers laughing at you, and worst of all, other criers assuming closeness and seeking you out.

'I know how you feel,' a scar-faced emaciate had said to him the previous day.

He'd looked back and thought, 'No, you don't.'

For the whole two weeks, he'd been alone in his cell twenty-three hours a day. He spent the other hour walking in a concrete circle, wondering why he'd bothered to leave his cell at all – what with the rain, the hateful looks of the officers sitting watching, and the imminent threat of death from the toughs who circled the quadrangle like piranha.

He'd seen prisons like Sandhill on television, but he hadn't expected it to be quite so grim – five stone 'halls' in a row, each a cavernous rectangle bordered with closed steel doors three storeys high: brick and stone and steel, all hard and cold like the officers who dotted the landings.

Inside his cell was a bunk bed, a desk, a television, a junkie (invariably) and a toilet. Jeremy was thankful for the latter when he learnt that only two years earlier he'd have found a swirling bucket of shit instead.

For twenty-three hours each day Jeremy stared at either the television or the underbelly of the top bunk, and thought of Amanda.

*

Amanda, whose Scottish accent had lured him from one end of The Stoke and Ferret to the other, then from one end of the country to the other. She was sitting drinking cheap cider when he first clapped eyes on her, and by the end of the night she was dancing in Kensington Gardens and singing 'Flower of Scotland' louder rather than better.

'I have chocolate at mine,' Amanda said, flopping down on the grass beside Jeremy.

'Then we must go and get it,' he said, standing up and pulling her towards him.

The B & B was a small, grotty building nestled between two large hotels. Amanda unlocked the front door, led Jeremy through the hall, into the kitchen, and rummaged through the cupboards. There were baked beans, tinned tomatoes, bread, but no chocolate.

'You lured me here under false pretences,' Jeremy said.

'Indeed,' she replied, pushing him against the fridge and kissing him violently.

Jeremy fell asleep beside her later that night. And when they woke in the early hours they were surprised to find each other even more attractive sober, surprised also to find that they were naked and that a woman in her twenties was staring at them from her bed under the window.

'Hello,' Jeremy whispered, looking into Amanda's eyes.

'Hello,' Amanda replied.

'I've never met anyone quite like you,' Jeremy said.

'What does that mean?'

'It means I've never met anyone quite like you. Say my name.'

'What is it again?'

'Jeremy.'

'Jeremy,' she obeyed.

'Say it again.'

'Jeremy,' she said bluntly, then more softly, '. . . Jeremy.'

'Jeremy and Amanda . . .' he paused '. . . are being watched.'

The room-mate's cat-eyes were shining with unashamed voyeurism.

'Let's go get that chocolate!' said Amanda.

They got dressed and walked four blocks in search of Lion Bars and Crunchies. Eventually, a twenty-four-hour supermarket appeared and as if by magic it had Lion Bars, Crunchies and seven different types of condoms.

Jeremy was taken aback when they got to the B & B and Amanda put the Crunchie in his mouth before kneeling and putting the condom on his penis, because the woman in her twenties was still in the room, sleeping in her bed under the window, only two or three feet away.

Jeremy saw the room-mate wriggle and he tried to warn Amanda, but there was now a Lion Bar in his mouth, one which had been elsewhere first and which did not taste the better for it. He could not say, 'There's a geeky type over there, and we're naked except for a well-travelled chocolate bar.'

But he didn't need to warn her because Amanda knew the girl was there, knew she was pretending to be asleep in the bed but readying herself with the bristles of her soft rubber hairbrush.

'Sally?' Amanda said, but the girl's eyes remained shut. 'Sally?' Amanda said, crawling over to the bed under the window and placing her head under the duvet.

Jeremy was in love! He watched the bump under the duvet sway and grind and then watched the girl's head do the same, her eyes open now and beckoning him.

He was in love. What man wouldn't be?

'You'll never handle her,' the room-mate said flatly when Amanda left to ablute afterwards.

Jeremy covered himself up, suddenly self-conscious.

When Amanda came back in, she jumped onto the bed

with such energy that Jeremy found himself saying, 'I love you!'

She snuggled into him and wondered if he would be like every other guy – who loved the whacky side of her that fucked like crazy and jumped onto beds – but after a day or two started to find her insatiable desire for adventure exhausting and irritating.

But Jeremy wasn't scared off like the other guys. He didn't think she was crazy or whacky, just honest and spontaneous. If she wanted something, she found a way to get it.

'I want to drop *e* at the Chelsea Flower Show,' she said a few days after they met, and together they wandered through flowers so glorious they'd wanted to cry.

'I want to have chicken and champagne in Hyde Park at 5 a.m.,' she said, and so the bubbles rose with the sun.

And if she needed something, she asked for it.

'Please hold me.'

'Please make me some soup.'

'Please stand up and sing me a love song from beginning to end.'

Jeremy felt alive with her. They explored the city together. They went to the movies. They took buses to unknown places, breathed in the world, saw and did new things. He watched her jump naked onto the bed at least twenty times after their first encounter, and reckoned he could have watched her jump naked onto beds forever.

'You can have your own room!' Jeremy told her when she said she was getting sick of her room-mate a few weeks after they met. 'And separate washing baskets!'

Amanda moved into Jeremy's Islington flat the next day. Physically it wasn't hard. All she had was a rucksack filled with clothes that were stiff and fusty from three months of hand washing. Emotionally it was agony. Amanda was a runner, always on the go. She'd left her Glasgow home at the age of sixteen and moved to Edinburgh, then travelled around Europe, then Asia, then moved to London. A few months here, a few there, always leaving before interesting new friends became needy.

It was two months ago that she'd arrived at Liverpool Street. She got a part-time job doing manicures and had twice won employee of the month. It was fun, as fun as anywhere else, but she knew it started to concern her when her room-mate Sally, during a late-night conversation, declared Amanda to be 'the best friend I've ever had'. Amanda stayed awake all night with the worry of it.

It wasn't that she was seriously damaged by any childhood trauma, or that she had no family, or a bad one. Quite the contrary. It was something else that made her drift. Some unfinished business in Glasgow that was too hard to face, for now.

But then she met Jeremy, and everything changed. He was a wonderful combination of danger and safety and he made her feel ready to face anything.

He looked after her, bought her things and took her places. 'I'll pick you up,' he'd say, after her evening shift at the salon, and he'd always be on time, parked in his Alpha with his music on and a big smile as she walked towards him in her short white uniform.

'I'll make you dinner,' he'd say, and the meal would be delicious and beautifully presented.

Jeremy wasn't just paternal. He was exciting: he liked driving fast on country roads, walking bare-foot through fields, and he greeted her unusual ideas with enthusiasm. He was clever: he read poetry and *The Observer* and enjoyed discussing issues over dinner. He was handy: he knew how to make things, and in fact presented Amanda with a beautiful hand-crafted chestnut jewellery box on their one-week anniversary. Not least, he was sexually daring: he knew about Purr Parties, held in the homes of the members, where single girls went to meet couples. The two of them went several times in the two months that they weren't married and made rules – never one without the other, the third always jointly chosen.

So Amanda was in love too. What girl wouldn't be? A rich property developer, tall and blond, handsome and not averse to rimming. She wondered how she'd had managed to pull him. She couldn't wait till her family and friends met him. They wouldn't believe what she'd managed. A drifter like her, with him!

'Will you marry me?' Jeremy asked only seven weeks after the night of the Lion Bar.

And that was that.

Soon after, they tied the knot in a register office in Camden. And that night Amanda jumped naked onto the Savoy Super Kingsize bed and said: 'I'm taking you to Glasgow!'

SIX

I planned my afternoon to a perfection. First, visit sex offender's parents' house. Second, attend pre-release case conference for said sex offender. Third, interview Jeremy Bagshaw.

Mr James Marney's parents lived in a high-rise flat on the south of the city. All four other high-rises were boarded up, ready for demolition, and number 99 – having thus far escaped the battlefield of rejuvenation – lay wounded in the middle. The Marneys lived on the thirteenth floor, so I had two options: dodge the shit and needles on the stairs, or take my chances in the lift. I chose latter, staring at the buttons as they failed to light up, and praying the doors wouldn't open en route to let someone get in to stare at me, rob me, smash me over the head.

I exited safely at the thirteenth floor, and walked the scabby corridor until I found number 13/7. It took a while for Mrs Marney to answer the door, and when she did she didn't open it very far. She was a clean, earthy-looking woman in her sixties. Before responding to my introduction, she closed the door even further and yelled to her husband: 'Frank, the social work's here! Frank! Social work!' Through the tiny crack in the door, she checked my ID card very thoroughly and asked repeatedly about the reasons for my visit. A moment later, her husband Frank, not so earthy-looking (angry, I'd say, scary even), came to the door and ushered me inside.

The flat was a shock after the filth of the lift and landing. It was neat and perfectly clean, with prints of hunting scenes on the wall, embroidered cloths on the arms of the couch, and a ridiculously large television set complete with DVD player and a huge collection of movies in the corner. I'd done loads of home visits in child protection, so I knew the score – surprise visits are often more fruitful, don't accept crusty mugs of tea or coffee, sit on a non-fabric seat if possible, and take notice of everything. These rules in mind, I took out the list of questions I needed to ask, which Danny had kindly printed off for me, and fired away.

They lived alone. They were pensioners. They were more than happy for their son to live with them after his release. They had his room ready. They would co-operate with super-vision, as long as we phoned first. They had one other daughter – single, no children – who lived in the north of the city. They felt terrible for their son, who was not allowed to see his children unsupervised – James junior and Robert now lived with their maternal grandmother in Stirling. Oh, and they were absolutely sure he was innocent. James junior, they argued, had made a silly comment at nursery, and was then tricked into fabricating an elaborate tale. 'Just nonsense,' Mr Marney said. 'He's an excellent dad. Brought the kids up by himself after Margie died, God rest her.'

'You know you won't be able to have the children to visit while he's here, not unsupervised,' I said.

'We never see them,' said Mr Marney.

'Well, if you want to, we need to okay it first. The police will need to approve the address too, and visit regularly. You understand?' I said, scouring the room and taking note of the DVD collection.

'Aye, but there'll be no need.'

'Do you mind if I use the loo?' I asked.

This was one of the ploys I'd used in childcare. Find a way to snoop. As usual, it worked.

'You were saying you never see the kids,' I said, taking my non-fabric seat a few minutes later.

26

'Aye, it's a shame,' Frank said curtly.

'So it's you who uses Teletubbies toothbrushes?' I asked. 'And watches Pingu?' I gestured to the penguin, who was hiding among the pile of DVDs next to the gigantic television.

Their faces were white as I stood up. 'Can I see the bedrooms?'

Of course, they didn't want me to see the bedrooms.

Frank started yelling at me: 'Who the hell do you think you are, stopping a good man seeing his kids?'

Mrs Marney tried to escort me to the door.

The kids in the bedroom started crying, then James junior managed to get the door open.

'Hi, kids,' I said, peering into the bedroom where two gorgeous little boys had been hiding since my arrival. The room looked well lived-in, with bunk beds, Ikea children's furniture, clothing, and piles and piles of toys.

I didn't get a chance to explain what would happen next. Truth be known, I wasn't sure anyway. Mr Marney told me to get the hell out and slammed the door in my face.

I'm great at this job, I thought to myself as I headed off to Sandhill. This guy had intended to live with his children, his victims. He was happy to lie to social work, the parole board and the police, and he had the wholehearted support of his parents.

SEVEN

Sandhill gave me the shivers. I'd been there before, visiting Chas, and the smell and look of it made me ill to the stomach. Mothers with babies smoked at the front door, white vans drove in and out, ferrying men to or from court, grumpy visits officers checked names on sheets and escorted people into the visits area.

I gave my name and took a seat in the foyer between two cheery-looking women.

'How's he doing?' one of the women asked the other.

'Och, it's his first time,' she said. 'He'll be better next time.'

Another world, Sandhill. Normal to most of its visitors, an expected part of life.

Eventually, a young gum-chewing admin worker escorted me through the staff entrance, where my bags were scanned and my ID checked. I followed her along a pretty garden area with a smokers' hut, through a huge steel gate, past the halls and into a Portakabin.

In a small room, four men sat at a table. A prison social worker, a prison officer, a policeman and Mr James Marney.

Shit, he was already there. I had no time to prep the others about my home visit.

Mr Marney was just what I expected. He had what I call the paedophile aura, a yellowish colour that coated his smug, normal, good-guy respectability. When he looked at me, I felt as though he'd spotted a victim and could see my past a mile a way. He seemed to smirk at me. I hated him. I hated sitting next to him. I hated being anywhere near him.

The prison officer introduced everyone and began rambling on about how well Mr Marney had done in prison, completing group work for sex offenders, responding particularly well to the victim empathy module, getting on well with fellow inmates, and working hard in the joinery shed.

'Can I stop you there?' I interrupted. 'I'm just back from visiting the proposed release addressed.' I gestured to the police officer. 'I understand you haven't been out there yet? It's clear Mr Marney's children are living with his parents.'

Penetrating Mr Marney's yellow cloud with steely eyes that warned *I am no victim*, I continued. 'You and your family appear to have misled us, and because of this it seems improbable that you would co-operate with supervision. Also, in my opinion, releasing you to the given address would place James and Robert at a very high risk of harm.'

The prison officer and the prison social worker were shocked. The police officer smiled from his end of the table. He looked like a forty-year-old Sean Connery but his voice was unfortunately very squeaky, which let the whole 007 thing down a wee bit.

'My, my. Is that so?' squeaked PC Bond.

What followed was an uncomfortable interrogation by Bond that eroded Marney's calm, and his story, piece by piece.

I never knew . . . They must've been visiting . . . The in-law's are arseholes . . . I wouldn't let them stay there . . . They miss me . . . They love me . . . I never touched them . . . He's fucking lying . . . Why the hell can't I live with my own kids? Why should I find somewhere else to live?

'Well done, Krissie,' said Bond on the way out of the case conference.

'Cheers,' I said.

The prison social worker, Bob, escorted me back over to the Agent's visits area. He was beautifully dressed and very well groomed, and he knew everyone. En route, we spotted the Priest, the Rabbi and the Minister, who were walking back from lunch.

'So what's the punch line?' he asked them.

Bob schmoozed the gate staff as we entered the main foyer, and spoke so rudely to the receptionist that I thought she might kill him ('Love the skirt! Primark or TK Max?'). Instead of killing him, she simply slapped him on the arm with a 'See *you*!'. Bob obviously had a way with people. He could tell the receptionist he'd shagged her husband and get a laugh. Mind you, he probably had.

Bob left me to wait in the Agents area to interview Jeremy Bagshaw. With my first pre-release meeting fresh in my mind, I felt on top of the world, ready for anything.

Hell, I was shit hot.

EIGHT

Jeremy Bagshaw was thinking about the day he and Amanda got married – a happy, perfect day – when his cell-mate, Billy, plonked his head down from the top bunk and said, 'Give me your banana.'

Billy, a bony waif with goggle eyes, had arrived a week earlier. He was rattling, cold turkey, his £60 a day habit rudely interrupted. During his first three days as Jeremy's co-pilot, Billy had moaned like a cat on the top bunk, shaking both beds with his itching, fogging the room with the stench of his chemical sweat.

'Shh!' Jeremy had said, exasperated after three days of hell.

'You want me to shut up, then give me something to trade with,' Billy replied.

'Just have a bit of respect,' Jeremy suggested.

A second later, Billy pounced down from his bed and grabbed Jeremy by the scruff of his polo shirt, his face too close, his mouth foaming.

'You want me to shut up, then help me,' said Billy, pushing Jeremy to the floor then grabbing five quid from his pocket.

After that, Billy stole each and every bit of Jeremy's allowance and/or canteen to swap for Valium, heroin, anything, so that sometimes the groaning and shaking stopped, but not for long. Some of the prisoners talked to their lawyers about how de-toxing in Sandhill was a violation of human rights and they wanted to sue the bastards. And it had to be said that coming off junk without medication, counselling or support was a right pain.

Billy would have joined the campaign and called his lawyer too, but he was too busy raising currency for gear. So far, his friend's sister had brought in five ten-pound bags of heroin by hiding it in her baby's nappy. (The officers weren't allowed to search babies.) He'd also befriended an officer, who'd given him cannabis at a grossly inflated price that his best friend on the outside had agreed to pay. So he was getting by, just.

At first, Jeremy let the pillaging of his allowance and food supplies happen rather than face the prospect of gang rape in the showers or being slashed with a toothbrush laden with melted razor blades. But he was hungry, and he wanted his banana at 14:15.

'Give me your banana.'

Jeremy only had one banana, and he intended to eat it at 14:15, after exercise.

'No.'

'Gimme the fucking banana.'

'Get your own banana,' said Jeremy in his dangerously posh English accent.

Billy pulled his head back onto the bed, the argument over, for now.

'Agents!' It was the boss, the gallery officer, and Jeremy snapped to, unsure what this meant.

'Social work or lawyer,' Billy informed him, reaching down for the banana.

'Could you mind this for me?' Jeremy asked the boss, snatching the fruit before Billy managed to get to it.

The look on the officer's face suggested the negative, so Jeremy flung the banana back on his bed to be swooped by the rattling vulture.

Jeremy knew better than to complain at this stage. The officer wouldn't give a shit, might even be irritated. And an irritated officer was a far more serious prospect than a missing banana.

So he put his shirt on and followed the officer out of the cell, down two flights of ancient worn wooden stairs, along the main hall that was guarded at first-floor level with an iron net. The net wasn't to stop suiciders from dying, Jeremy reckoned, but from hitting floor-level staff on the head. It worked, apparently. No staff had been injured by falling debris for years.

There'd been a jumper the week before.

'Code Blue!' the officer had yelled. Alarms had gone off and keys had jingled as staff ran to the hall. Then all was still and closed for hours, until the hall door opened and there was a small black van parked in front, with a small man in black standing beside it, waiting.

A pounding noise had come from the cell next to Jeremy's. A deep boom-boom-boom of fist against metal door, and then another, and another, until two hundred metal doors were thumping with the fists of the grieving, thumping a goodbye to the body that was being liberated into a small black van.

Jeremy waited underneath the suicide net while other prisoners were rounded up for transporting, and when they were all marked out and counted, he followed the officer into the concrete quadrangle, past D hall and through a nondescript door that led almost to the real world. 'Bagshaw!' an officer yelled, and Jeremy let himself be identified and escorted into the interview room.

The woman was about the same age as Amanda, Jeremy thought – twenty-eight, give or take. She had thick layered hair and an enchanting smile. Natural. Her face was beautiful – fresh and honest – and she wore surprisingly casual and trendy clothes compared with the lawyers in the other rooms – well-cut jeans, cute shirt, fitted jacket, boots with a bit of a heel.

'My name's Krissie Donald. How are you getting on?' she said, shaking his hand and looking him in the eye before sitting down.

Krissie explained that the High Court had requested a pre-trial report for background information so that if he was found guilty he could be sentenced straight away. She couldn't discuss the offence, just background stuff. And she couldn't do the report unless he consented. Did he consent?

Jeremy was surprised by her. The prison staff he'd been in contact with had either worn gloves or initiated well-rehearsed routines for hand-shaking avoidance (one hand on the door handle, the other pointing to the chair – 'Take a seat Mr Bagshaw'). He understood why – most hands in prison were wrapped firmly around sticky penises 24/7. He wouldn't want to shake hands either.

But Krissie Donald had, and it'd been nice to feel a warm, if rather sweaty, palm in his, like a normal everyday human being.

Krissie asked what he liked to be called. Was Jeremy all right? She asked if he was coping inside, if he was feeling okay, eating, sleeping? If he'd had any visitors? Any news from home? She asked things he wished she hadn't, because when he answered he cried, and it wasn't okay to cry in Sandhill. It was the opposite.

NINE

What a buzz, meeting Jeremy Bagshaw. Like the initial flush of romance – intimate and intense. I wasn't aware at the time but if I'd asked any of my office mates they'd have told me that, like romance, after a while the excitement would dwindle, amazing stories would lose their zing and you would find yourself wanting to tell them to just stop it for God's sake and close that door on your way out.

The thing that immediately stood out about Jeremy Bagshaw was that he was extremely good-looking. Of the 956 prisoners in Sandhill, I would have put money on him being the only one with a healthy weight – not eaten away by heroin or stuffed by the fried carbs that had replaced it. And he was rare in having hair that wasn't oily from the forsaking of a twice-weekly shower; nails that were clean; eyes that were bright and free of sand. All in hall, he was a bit of a Russell Crowe hunk, actually.

Compared to sitting next to the lying-creepo-lewd-and-libber, it felt much more comfortable talking to Jeremy. No sticky aura. No sickly stare that made me feel exposed. I shook his hand without thinking about the alphabets of hepatitis on offer at Sandhill. And as I looked him in the eye, I saw something vulnerable and scared.

Jeremy had been on remand for two weeks. That meant he'd spent two weeks in a grotty cell with different 'co-pilots', one after another, locked up twenty-three hours a day. The only perk for remand prisoners is the possibility of a daily visit, instead of three a month like convicted prisoners. But this perk was irrelevant in Jeremy's case because no

35

one had visited him. He hadn't even spoken to anyone on the phone in all that time.

He told me he was fine, that it was his choice not to have contact with Amanda. He didn't feel up to it, he said, which wasn't unusual for men in his situation, diving into his time and hiding in it. He'd thrown out Amanda's daily letters because it was too hard to read them, he told me, his blue eyes heavy with tears that he was about to let go.

I didn't want him to start crying. A crying client would be problematic. I'd have two choices: to be a heartless bastard, ignore his tears, and move the conversation on by saying: 'Would you like me to come another time?'; or to give him a hug, thereby relinquishing all authority and professionalism and rendering myself a soft touch.

So I did everything I could to stop the tears, defaulting into my particular brand of cheery empathy, telling him a bit about my own despairing moments and turning the page on them. I didn't tell him an unprofessional amount about myself, mind, just this and that, to put him at ease, open him up. And it clearly worked because he talked for two hours. I'd been warned by my colleagues that they regularly did two-hour-long interviews and I'd wondered how they could possibly manage it, sitting there on a chair in a smelly room asking open questions, reflecting things back, maintaining a non-threatening, non-judgemental posture that also exuded professional distance and authority. But with Jeremy I found myself so interested in everything he said that the minutes flew by.

His work as a property developer fascinated me for a start. I'm an uncashed-up and unfulfilled real estate junkie, who wastes far too much of my time watching crap housing renovation shows, one after the other, and dreaming of that place in Spain with the veranda and one of those pools that merge into the horizon so it looks like you can swim in the sky. That said, I hadn't even managed to re-do the bathroom of my flat in all the years I'd lived there. Hence I was very impressed with Jeremy, who owned seven flats around London, and had two renovation projects on the go and three full-time employees.

'How do you manage getting workmen to turn up?' I asked him, drawing on my sofa-based knowledge.

'There are ways,' he said. 'Chocolate digestives work a treat.'

His relationship with Amanda had clearly been passionate, although he didn't speak about her much, except to say she was wonderful and he'd do anything to protect her. This was why he'd refused visits – to protect her from this place.

His hobbies included cycling, running, Thai cooking, reading (he could never get through a James Joyce, like me), watching movies (his favourite, like mine, was *The Shawshank Redemption*).

And his childhood had been heart-wrenchingly terrible.

When I asked him about growing up, his head dropped down and swayed from left to right a little. After a moment, he attempted to say something.

'What was that?' I hadn't deciphered his mumble.

'I, um . . .' he whimpered, head still down and shaking.

'Are you all right?' I asked.

He dragged his head upwards, lips quivering, let out a deep breath, then looked at me.

'When I was four, I did something really terrible. It's why I'm in here, it's what they have on me, a history of violence, because I tried to stop my sister from crying and I . . . I accidentally killed her, when I was four.'

I was used to people telling me private stuff – stuff they'd never told anyone and were surprised to be telling me. I think I have the right kind of face, or ask the right questions anyway. I'm always being told things out of the blue – I stole my mum's television, or I punched my husband, or I slept with Giuseppe from the gym, or I have a terrible itchy genital disease – but this topped anything I'd ever been told before and I didn't quite know how to react. What did you say to someone who killed his baby sister? 'Tell me, how did it feel to murder your sister?'

My mind was reeling. I was aware I'd relinquished my blank, non-judgemental social work face and instead had a horror-stricken open-mouthed one that screamed JESUS CHRIST, YOU DID WHAT?

He broke down and cried onto the cold desk between us, and I felt like crying too. It was too awful, what he'd done. His little sister was gone. And he'd paid for it ever since.

Before I could decide on how to respond to his tears, he managed to compose himself, thank me, ask me to please come and see him again, and then leave the room. If he hadn't done this, I think I'd have sat there forever not knowing what to say, looking at his head rocking in his hands. The man I was visiting had accidentally killed a baby, destroying the lives of everyone he loved, and his own life too, when he was four years old – only a tiny bit older than my little Robbie.

Gathering my notes after he left the room, I realised I'd only written a few lines.

Name: Jeremy Bagshaw
Date of birth: 21/7/1976
Address: 67 Station Street, Islington, London
Currently on remand in HMP Sandhill, Glasgow
Charge: Murder

TEN

Chas assured me everything was hunky-dory at home, so I left work early with my colleagues and we went off to a West End pub to celebrate my first day in the job.

I'd been marvelling at Danny all day, watching his every move. He dressed immaculately, seemed more confident and at ease than anyone I knew, and was the funniest bastard I'd ever met.

In the taxi, he told me he'd written a social enquiry report for a stalker. In the section about the offender's use of time, the report had read: 'Mr Jones enjoys surfing the net and wanking his dog in the park.'

'Sheriff Ross hates social workers. So he hauls me into the court,' Danny said, 'and threatens me with contempt.'

'It was obviously a typo,' Danny had explained to the Sheriff. 'The report should read "walking".'

'Stop here,' said Danny to the taxi driver, somehow knowing that we'd reached our destination. 'Just drop us at the corner, that'll be fine.'

As Danny got out of the cab, extended his stick and retrieved money from his wallet, the taxi driver noticed he was blind.

'So do you just listen to music, then?' the driver asked Danny as he counted out the change.

'Aye, I just listen to music and that, you know,' Danny replied, entering into a conversation about Glasgow bands to make the driver feel at ease.

Later he told me about a catalogue of similar incidents involving people's bizarre reactions to his disability.

One evening, he'd been walking home from the Sheriff Court, where he'd given evidence about a drug dealer he'd supervised. He said he could smell the shit-caked clothes of the two drunks a mile away. They were lying under the bridge, clutching their quarter bottles of fortified wine with all their might, when Danny passed by with his stick.

'And we think we've got it bad,' said Jakey 1.

'There but for the grace of God,' said his friend.

I was no better. In the pub that night, I was wondering how much the general opinion of me depended on my looks, which were, I had to admit, rather good.

'Do you want to touch my face?' I asked Danny when Robert went to the bathroom.

'What?'

'You can touch my face if you like,' I said.

If he touched my face, I supposed, he would understand that my wit and intelligence were accompanied by the kind of symmetrical features that babies and jurors like.

'Do I have to?' he asked, and then, when Robert returned to the bar:

'You'll never guess what . . . she wants me to touch her face!'

'Can I?' asked Robert, doing it anyway, and all was raucous for several Krissie-is-a-dick-filled minutes.

Idiot.

Changing the subject, I told them all about my triumphant detective work with the sex offender, and then about Jeremy. 'He seems sad . . . and nice,' I said.

'That's the murder one, yeah?' said Danny. 'Doesn't seem too nice to me.'

'He's not guilty yet,' I asserted. 'Anyway, I think it's important to get to know a client before looking at what other people say about them, or accuse them of.'

'Noble,' said Robert.

'Impossible,' added Danny.

40

They didn't seem overly interested in Jeremy's childhood story. 'But have you ever heard anything as sad as that?' I asked.

'Aye!' Robert said, and went on to top my story with one involving an old bloke with dementia and his three-legged terrier. He and Danny then played sad-story poker, bidding one tale of woe after the other.

Danny had supervised the shoplifting daughter of a notorious serial killer. She'd blamed herself for years for failing to alert the authorities to her father's activities, before turning to heroin.

Robert was supervising a guy who got into an argument with the neighbours, lashed out with a hammer, and accidentally killed a young girl who just happened to be walking up the close.

One of Danny's lifers was a prostitute who had failed in her plan to kill herself, but had managed to take out her kids.

And so it went on. I realised that Jeremy's was just one of many, many sad stories of prisoners' lives.

'After a week or so you'll stop talking about your cases,' said Danny. 'You'll get home and be like – yeah, yeah, work was fine. You'll get used to it.'

'If you don't, you'll get constant migraines, like Hilary,' added Robert.

'Or be on long-term sick, like a third of us,' said Danny.

'Divorced like two thirds of us,' Robert nodded, obviously divorced.

'Alcohol-dependent like three quarters . . .' Danny raised his glass to mine.

'Welcome to the job!' I said, clinking glasses with two fragments of social work wreckage.

When I arrived home that night I'd have sworn burglars had ransacked the place. Clothes were all over the floor of the hall, the bath was filled with scum-topped grot, the toilet was

41

un-flushed, dishes were piled on the kitchen table and on the sink, and all the cushions from my new Habitat sofa were piled up in the spare bedroom. I was about to scream in anger – *How could the place be so messy after just one day?* – when Chas and Robbie pounced out at me from behind the bedroom curtain. Robbie looked so happy and chortled so hard that I forgave Chas for his housekeeping skills this time. As my job got harder and my hours longer, it became an issue that I was far less reasonable about.

The painting had gone well, Chas told me. They'd managed an elaborate multicoloured train track covering half the floor of the studio, and spent the rest of the day singing nursery rhymes with the sculptors (Robbie was a big hit with the sculptors).

'Did you get any work done?' I asked Chas.

'Tomorrow,' he said. 'We're both going to paint the sea.'

Chas had made pizzas, hence the crap everywhere and the dishes in the sink, because unlike most sensible first-worlders, who either have pizzas delivered or buy supermarket ones, Chas made his from scratch. What this meant was two hours shopping, one hour kneading, another hour tossing and rolling, another chopping toppings, and another carefully placing ingredients on top. What this also meant was that every surface in the kitchen was covered in flour, every dish and every piece of cutlery was dirty and not in the dishwasher, radios were on all over the flat (he liked to cook while listening to the radio), and I didn't eat till 10.30 p.m. As I tried to sleep through the indigestion, I wondered when the right time would be to tell Chas that I hated pizza.

Later that night, after Robbie had fallen asleep, I gazed at him and tried to imagine a little boy the same age as him – someone who couldn't even put on his own shoes – killing someone. If Robbie had killed a three-week-old baby, could he possibly know what he was doing? Would he have it in him to make that kind of decision? Could you even call it killing? How would I cope if my own baby died in that way?

The next day I posted the home background report for James Marney. As I walked back into my office, Robert was blue with laughter, having just received a medical certificate from his GP. Being six foot six, his desk had caused him back and leg pain for months. Robert had spoken to Hilary about getting a larger desk, who had spoken to the criminal justice admin officer, who had spoken to her admin senior, who'd filled out a form and given it to her team leader, who'd attached the form and written an accompanying letter to the man in charge of the disability fund, who'd read over the rules and regulations regarding special office equipment, photocopied the correspondence thus far, set up a meeting with his boss, and phoned Robert with the outcome: 'Yes, you may have a large desk under the disability budget, but we require a medical certificate from your GP.'

So Robert had spoken to his GP, a pleasant and witty woman in her late twenties. The medical certificate had just arrived in the post and this was the reason for Robert's crippling laughter. Robert handed me the piece of paper. It read: 'This is to certify that Mr Robert Brown is tall.'

But enough of the hilarity. I had to go to Sandhill.

While I was waiting for Jeremy to arrive, I realised that Danny and Robert were right. It was daft and impossible to resist reading about the offence. So I pored over the only piece of paper that had been provided for me – the indictment.

JEREMY ANDREW BAGSHAW, Prisoner of Sandhill, Glasgow, you are indicted at the instance of the right honourable THE LORD JOHNSTONE OF LOCHABER, Her Majesty's Advocate, and the charge against you is that on Sunday 6 April, at The Lock House, By Crinan, Arygll, you did assault Bridget McGivern and did sever her breasts with a knife or similar instrument and did stab her on the body and repeatedly on the neck with a knife or similar instrument and you did murder her.

It hit me. As I waited for him to arrive, I realised that Jeremy Bagshaw might well be good-looking and middle-class, he might well be in love and have a tear-jerking childhood story, but he'd also been accused of chopping off a woman's breasts and stabbing that woman in the body and in the neck. And the blood was probably spurting all over the wall of the cottage in Crinan while he looked on with bloodstained teeth . . .

'Hello.'

It was my murderer. He had a black eye, and he didn't look like someone who could stab a woman and cut off her breasts. I wanted to ask him about the victim. Who was she? What was the connection? But I wasn't allowed to discuss the offence, and Jeremy looked frightened. He'd been seriously beaten.

'What happened?'

'Nothing,' he answered, looking over my shoulder nervously.

'You can tell me,' I whispered.

'Nothing,' he whispered back.

I spent a while trying to coax it out of him, pointing out the anti-bullying poster on the wall and so on. But he was scared. He kept checking to see who was in the other interview rooms. I was savvy enough to know that being beaten is bad, but being a grass is worse, so I didn't push him.

'Don't tell anyone. Especially Amanda. I don't want to worry her,' he said.

'I don't need to speak to Amanda for this type of report,' I said.

'You'd like her,' he said, recalling how he'd fallen head

over heels in love with her the first time he saw her. She'd had such a captivating smile, he said, and she laughed a lot. He loved that about her, the way she laughed.

'Please don't tell her I'm having a hard time, promise? Please don't talk to her,' he pleaded.

ELEVEN

Amanda took Jeremy to Glasgow a week after the wedding. They drove fast from London but slowed a little somewhere after Penrith when Amanda gave Jeremy a blowjob.

After five hours on the road, Scotland appeared by way of an insignificant white sign. Amanda shuddered. Ten whole years away, not far away for most of it, but far enough to be a whole other world.

Jeremy might have shuddered too if he'd known he was about to meet Amanda all over again. No longer just Amanda, wild and whacky. No longer Amanda, role-less and un-referenced. She would be a daughter and a school friend and an ex-colleague. She would have an old primary school and photo albums and a favourite café. And Jeremy would be checked out by Amanda's significant others outside his zone.

Jeremy had never been to Glasgow, but as they drove in it was everything he'd imagined. Heavy impenetrable cloud hovered somewhere just above his windscreen, grey high-rises lined the road, sometimes painted at the front to try and give a good impression, but mostly not. Large blue signs pointed left to Glasgow, straight ahead to Glasgow, right to Glasgow. Glasgow was all around, the 'dear green place' with no dearness in sight and no green, just a confusion of signs pointing in every direction that seemed to say: 'If you don't know where you are, then what the fuck are you doing here?'

They drove past the dense West End and along the Great Western Road, with huge trees, flowers in the middle and beautiful Victorian town houses on either side. Jeremy felt uplifted. This was better. But then the houses got littler and the flowers more shrivelled, and then Amanda pointed and he turned into a dowdy street filled with badly maintained boxes.

'This is us!' she said, outside number 43, and he stopped the car and kissed her on the lips and wondered if the girl who had grown up in this house was the same girl who had sucked his dick somewhere between Penrith and Carlisle.

Amanda's parents were older than he expected – approaching seventy, maybe – and nicer. Mrs Kelly was round and short, with thick grey hair, a lifetime of smiles lining her face. Her husband – slim, fit, moustached and Brylcreemed – was less smiley, but no less lovable. They hugged their girl ('Oh, my darling girl!' her mother said over and over), they hugged him ('Welcome to the family, son!') and they served soup that had been simmering since Amanda phoned ten miles after Motherwell.

The house was a four-room box filled with Amanda memorabilia – ballet photos, badminton trophies, beauty college certificates – and it smelt nice. Jeremy noticed that everything about Amanda seemed different once they walked through the door; her clothes changed from bright and bohemian to old-fashioned and comfortable, her chat from urban and hip to giggly, gossipy. Jeremy wasn't sure how he felt about the changes initially.

After a no-nonsense dinner of lamb stew, Amanda's mother put on some old family videos. They drank beer as they watched Amanda performing in her Primary Three nativity play with chubby grin. They laughed as she long-jumped in the school sports aged eleven, and as she poked out her tongue while sunbathing on holiday in Portugal aged fourteen.

All four were getting a little tipsy as they pored over old report cards . . .

Could do better.
Lacks concentration.

Seems bored . . . and were positively pissed when the photo of Amanda and her first boyfriend, Peter Bishop, found its way onto the coffee table.

'Oh God, what was I thinking?' Amanda said, examining the fifteen-year-old boy. He was very good-looking. Her comment had obviously been intended to put Jeremy at ease.

'What *were* you thinking?' someone said. The voice was not a happy one.

'What you were you thinking, Mand? Disappearing like that?'

Her mother was drunk enough to confront her now.

'Ten years without coming back. And there were times we thought you might be dead!'

Amanda put the photo album and the beer down on the coffee table, walked over to where her mother was sitting, knelt before her, and buried her head in her lap.

'I'm so sorry,' Amanda wept. 'I don't know what I was thinking! I love you! I know it sounds corny, but I wanted to try and find myself.'

'And did you?'

'I found Jeremy,' Amanda replied. 'I'm sorry I hurt you.'

Amanda's father joined his girls on the sofa while Jeremy watched with a tear in his eye.

They spent three days organising a party to celebrate their marriage. Jeremy mostly managed to keep his mobile switched off, even though his second-in-charge was having a nervous breakdown. The glass from Germany had arrived for the patio doors in the Finsbury Park project but was the wrong size. And the water pipes in one of the cheaper rentals had burst, damaging the immaculate dining room belonging to the gay couple downstairs.

'Send the glass back,' Jeremy said. 'We won't pay unless it's what we ordered. Then ring the plumber and the insurers. Easy.'

The party was at to be held the Grantly Hotel, a three-star job two blocks further into pebble-dash hell, and Mand's parents were insisting on paying for it.

'We won't hear of it!' Mr Kelly had said when Jeremy opened his wallet. 'It's the least we can do for our Mand.' Jeremy had never conceived of shortening Amanda's beautiful name, but there it was – Mand.

At first, Jeremy wasn't sure how he felt as the pieces of Amanda began to click into place. *Mand.* Who was she?

They went for drinks at a West End pub. Amanda's friends gathered around a table and fired questions at her. What have you been doing? Why didn't you write at least? How did you two meet? Did you know Peter Bishop is divorced already? Jeremy drank it all in – how bohemian and unselfconscious the pub was, how much they all loved Amanda, how bubbly she was in their company. He had a great night, and he worked the crowd so thoroughly that they all approved of him wholeheartedly by the time they left.

That night he and Amanda kissed in bed and didn't stop for hours.

'I think I love you more than I did before we arrived,' he told her.

'I've been a bad daughter.'

'They forgive you. They love you. And I love everything about you.'

He loved that she was wildly spontaneous but could also slob on the sofa for hours watching *Anne of Green Gables*. He loved her family and her roots. Most of all, he loved her willingness to tear herself away from them and start afresh with him in London.

At the wedding party, Jeremy smiled at his wife, the pieces of her together now, complete.

Red swirling carpet, twenty large round tables and a teensy DJ. At least thirty over-seventies drinking beer faster than at least fifty under-thirties. Small children running in circles on a larger-than-necessary dance floor, and a cauldron of mince on a table beside a cauldron of mashed spud.

Jeremy loved mashed spud, and when he saw the cauldron he nearly cried because it reminded him of his best and earliest memory.

The party had all the perfect ingredients:

A groping drunk uncle.

A father's moving speech – 'We were given this girl from God, and every day we thank him.'

A tearful mother who used her daughter's inebriation as a good opportunity to make Amanda promise never to disappear again like that! To come back twice a year at least, keep in contact. 'Promise me, Mand! Promise me!' she said.

'I promise!' Amanda said. And she meant it. Her desire to flee had diminished since she met Jeremy.

The circle at the end spun fast around them, Auld Lang Syne, in and out, in and out, and it took hours for them to say goodbye to everyone because everyone had SO much to say.

I love you

Don't tell anyone but you are my favourite cousin.

You're much nicer than that Peter Bishop, who's divorced already!

Mate, you're a lucky bastard!

Goodbye, son.

Goodbye, Dad.

Goodbye, Mum.

Amanda puked all the way to the end of the Great Western Road, up Loch Lomond, over the Rest-and-be-Thankful, through Inveraray and to the Crinan Canal. It was 3 a.m. by the time they arrived. Jeremy lifted her up and walked into the luxurious waterside lodge they'd rented for two weeks. Two whole weeks together reading books, walking, talking, cooking, fishing, making love. Bliss.

'Oh shite, I've barfed ma load on the hall carpet,' Amanda said, her accent now as strong as her breath.

'That's all right, my darling. I'll clear it up. Just you lie down and sleep.'

TWELVE

Throughout my life, when people have told me not to do something, I have had an overwhelming urge to do it.

'Don't look now!'

'Don't have sex on a first date.'

'Whatever you do, don't drink more than two glasses of this cocktail!'

'Please don't talk to Amanda,' Jeremy had said.

I fought it for a while, especially as there was no need whatsoever for me to visit Amanda. The report required half an hour's interview and half an hour's typing. Full stop. End of story. Should've finished it already.

But I was consumed with curiosity. What was his wife like? Did she still love him? Believe him innocent? Who was the victim, Bridget McGivern? Did Jeremy and/or Amanda know her?

As soon as I got back from the interview with Jeremy at Sandhill, I rang the salon Jeremy said she worked at. A very grumpy male boss answered the phone and then put her on. Amanda was desperate to hear news of her husband, but she was working late.

'Can you come in?' she asked, before arguing with her boss in the background. 'I'm going to do her nails!' I heard her say.

I hated manicures almost as much as I hated the mani-cured. From what I could see, they were mainly reserved for the section of society that had no use for hands, who sat for long periods waiting for polish to dry – wiggle and blow, wiggle and blow – for those who had more time than reasons to live, who had no need for typing, whose worst fear was the breaking of a nail.

As I walked into the Pine Tree Unisex Hairdressing Salon in Newton Mearns, my opinion of manicuring wasn't challenged as I beheld stationary ladies in lines, wiggling and blowing, wiggle and blow.

What was Amanda doing there? She was beautiful, skinny as a malinky, with thick red curly hair. Her clothes were bohemian and comfortable and her smile was captivating. If she wore make-up, it was impossible to tell. She was natural and flawless. If I'd seen her at a party, I'd have wanted to talk to her. My kind of girl. She looked way too interesting to be interested in nails.

Amanda seated me at her tiny table and dipped my hands into warm honey as I told her about the pre-trial report.

'How is he?' she asked.

Dilemma – he'd not only asked me not to talk to her, he'd also said he didn't want her to know he was having a hard time. I desperately wanted to tell her that he wasn't fine, that he was probably being bullied and might be in danger. But on the way to the salon I'd asked myself if I'd want to know in the same situation. If Chas was bruised and scared, would I want to know when all I could do was worry?

'He's fine,' I lied. 'He's coping. How about you? How are you coping?'

'I'm not,' she said, biting her lip. 'Of course I'm not. But Jeremy's innocent. I know he is. Did he tell you his mother won't corroborate his alibi? Fucking bitch. She wants him locked away. I don't know who killed Bridget but he didn't. A monster did.'

Definitely my kind of girl. Upfront, no-nonsense.

'My life has exploded in my face,' she said, looking at me and smiling kindly, 'and your nails are a bloody disaster.'

'Did you always want to be a nail technician?'

She laughed at this. 'I wanted to travel, and you can do this anywhere.'

We paused for some hand rituals – cleaning, drying, massaging – and I entered a dimension unknown to me before then, the anaesthetised state of the manicured, and my opinion of the ladies in lines began to change.

'I used to do Jeremy's nails, on the sofa at night. It was one of "our" things.' She took a brown leather case from her bag and touched it almost lovingly. 'He gave me this set to use, especially for him.'

The leather set was beautiful and had her initials burnt into it. AK. Inside were stainless steel implements of all shapes and sizes.

'Are you married?' she asked me, the remnants of my clipped nails falling onto her felt cloth.

'No,' I eventually answered, having given the question more thought than it required. I'd never thought of myself as the marrying type. I'd never wanted to waste ten grand on a party that I probably wouldn't enjoy with people I hardly knew. I'd never wanted to be the centre of attention, or to be given away like some Christmas hamper. Weddings made me cry, and not for the usual reasons. At my work pal Marj's I cried because her husband was a fuck-face. He always got pissed and then he pissed wherever he so pleased – I caught him peeing in my Sainsbury's basil plant one night, and Marj said one of 'his things' was to stand over her and let loose in the bath. Even more than that, he was a misogynist who only ever became animated when talking to other men about fucking-Celtic-this-and-UEFA-that. I don't think he ever looked me, or any other woman, in the eye. God knows his piss must've tasted like Lindt chocolate 'cause for the life of me I couldn't imagine why else Marj would have married him. I howled uncontrollably as she headed down the aisle to merge with her flabby lump of crusty urine.

Then there was my cousin's wedding in Skye. I cried at the that one 'cause I was so embarrassed. I'd asked a really cute guy called Jamie from Uni to accompany me there. I'd fancied him for months, but he was Mr Popular, awfully cute, good at everything, and rich. He agreed to come, and the sexual chemistry was so huge we couldn't talk to each other at all during the six-hour drive. We just sat there, our chemicals fizzing across his gear stick. I changed into a very sexy outfit and we raced to the church just in time for the ceremony. He followed me to our seats and when we sat down our bodies were so close I had goose bumps all over.

'You've got something stuck on your back,' he whispered in my ear.

'Thanks,' I replied, excited by the heat of his whisper. I reached round, but couldn't feel anything. 'Can you get it?' I asked. He didn't seem keen. 'Please,' I said, fluttering my eyelashes.

He put his hand behind my back. I heard a sticky-tape sound. Then he handed me the panty liner I'd removed before getting changed.

It was used.

Clatty, disgusting, idiot.

I was so overwhelmed with embarrassment that I began crying. Tears rolled down my cheeks as I scrunched the thing up and put it in my handbag.

I drank too much champagne while the photographs were being taken and ended up in the bed of my (single) hotel room before the speeches, moving my head from side to side to try and quell the pre-vomit spinning. The following day, we drove for six hours in silence again. Not because of our fizzing chemicals, but because the lovely Jamie thought I was a tosspot, and he was right.

So weddings weren't my big thing.

But when Amanda asked me if I was married, my entire body felt as though it'd been dipped in her hand-honey. Mmm, marriage. A public declaration of my love for Chas. An official merging of our families. Chas could officially become Robbie's father. We could love each other for eternity, officially. Who was I? What was I thinking? Why was I suddenly wanting things on paper? It didn't make sense, but the thought of marriage now seemed officially yummy. It was warm and romantic and nonsensically delicious. And I found myself wondering why Chas hadn't asked me to marry him. Why hadn't he invited me to the Rogano one night and gotten down on one knee and embarrassed me with his well-rehearsed speech? Why hadn't I leafed through wedding brochures and *Hello* magazines to find the perfect dress, the perfect hotel, the car, the piper and all that wedding shite?

'Where were you married?' I asked, returning from la-la land for a moment. I was interested in her, but I was also picturing different possibilities for me and Chas: the gloomy highland castle, the posh hotel; the marquee, the University Chapel, Gretna Green, Mum and Dad's back garden, Sri Lanka.

She didn't answer the question directly, but told me about their wedding party in Glasgow, when she introduced her find to the family. It was the happiest she'd ever been, she said, filing my nails.

'Where'd you go on your honeymoon?' Hmm, I thought. Where might Chas and I go? The great barrier reef? Kerala? On safari?

When Amanda told me the Lock House, on the Crinan canal in Argyll, I tried not to show my shock, because it was the place of the murder.

'Some honeymoon,' Amanda said. 'The first night I puked. And on the second day Jeremy was called down to London for an emergency. An A & E nurse rang to say his mother had been admitted to hospital with a suspected heart condition. The next time I saw him he'd been charged with murdering Bridget . . . my biological mother.'

'*Biological*?'

'She gave me up at birth. I was adopted.'

THIRTEEN

Chas and I had our first fight that evening.

For two years we'd smiled and kissed and said I love you at least once a day. We'd laughed together over elaborate bedtime stories in Robbie's room, then snuggled after dinner on the sofa while making various forms of physical contact. In the week before my job, I'd also crammed in an inordinate number of battery-induced orgasms and we'd started to consider ways to one day integrate Chas into the procedure.

But when I got home that night, our happy loving routine flew out the window.

'Jesus!' I said instead of hello. 'Why is the hall wall covered in cake mix?'

'It's not cake mix,' Chas said. 'We were making a potion!'

'The washing basket is overflowing, there's no food in the fridge. And why haven't you asked me to marry you?'

'Do you want to get married?' Chas asked. 'If you want to, then we can,' he said, which made me get on the defensive.

Confusing myself as much as Chas, I told him of course I didn't want to get married. Who needs a bit of paper? Marriage was old fashioned and a sure way to stuff up a good thing and anyway, what sort of girl hangs around waiting for a guy to ask her, like that's the only way it can happen? 'It's pathetic!' I said, with a tone that made Chas wish he'd been gay.

I did synchronised huffing, tidying and apologising, and in the end Chas did the sensible thing and went for a walk while I put Robbie to bed and filled my stomach with the (cleverly hidden) dinner he'd made. And even though pizza didn't warrant meal-status like the leg of lamb I'd been dreaming about all day, the one I'd asked him to take out of the freezer and cook with rosemary, it filled a void. So by the time Chas got home I was ready to give him a huff-free apology.

'Thanks for dinner,' I said. 'I'm crazy, aren't I?'

'A bit.'

'I met this woman today and she started talking about her wedding, and I felt all gooey about it. It doesn't make sense. It's not me.'

'I like it when you're all gooey,' he said, kissing my neck.

'But it's not me, is it, Chas? I think my job's upsetting me. God, the stories I hear are unbelievable,' I said, filling him in on my cases so far. 'And being full time sucks. We've no time to have fun, have we? I don't blame you if you go off me.'

He sat me down.

'I've been thinking,' he said. 'The whole idea of a love story being "boy meets girl, boy loses girl, boy gets girl back" is bollocks. It's not a line that starts then ends. It's a circle. You meet, you lose, you meet, you lose, you meet and it goes on and on, round and round. We're meeting each other again just now. Learning new stuff. I'm trying to put an exhibition together. You've just started a really difficult job and you miss Robbie, and I'm pleased to meet you, Krissie! I'm going to learn something new about you, and I'm going to fall in love with you all over again.'

I didn't have a clue what he was talking about with all his circles and lines. God, sometimes living with an artist was exhausting.

'I don't think my bad mood is really about us, Chas. I'm just worried about the pre-trial report case, Jeremy. He's being beaten, maybe even raped, and I don't know who to tell.'

'Don't get emotionally involved,' he told me. 'Ask any

doctor or psychiatrist . . . it's *the* rule.' He knew what he was talking about, after his stint in Sandhill.

'The prison oozes tragedy. The trick is to not let it seep into you. You have to keep a distance. When I was there, I sometimes imagined a protective shield surrounded me . . . like Get Smart's cone of silence or Violet Incredible's spherical force field. Sounds daft, but it worked. Look after number one,' he said, 'and two and three. That's us, this family. Okay?'

'Okay. I promised I'd go see his wife again tomorrow . . . But I'll take my protective cone.'

'Who'd you promise?'

'Her.'

'Why?'

'She's upset.'

'No social worker visited my girlfriend twice when I was due in court.'

'Did you have a girlfriend?' Chas had always been very vague about his exes. I knew he used to shag around a lot, but he told me he never got too involved with anyone 'cause he was 'waiting for Mrs Donald'.

'That's not the point. Don't visit people unless you have to.'

I didn't push him about the ex-girlfriend thing. I didn't want to start imagining him kissing someone else on the neck, loving someone else. This kind of probing had driven many a woman round the bend. So with my issue of the day seemingly resolved, I moved on to Chas's. He was having a ball with Robbie, but he told me that day he had bitten the bullet and booked a date for his first ever exhibition.

'I'm terrified,' he admitted.

'You're a genius. I know you are. It'll be fantastic.'

But his time was limited. And Chas's cunning plan to paint and parent was (surprise, surprise) proving a disaster. So far,

Robbie's (very cute) handprints had made their way onto three of Chas's masterpieces.

Robbie was ready for some socialising anyway, so we decided to get him into a nursery three hours each morning, for Mum and Dad to look after him three afternoons a week, and for me to cut down on Marks & Spencer's treats and make room in our budget for a cleaner.

So when Chas went off to paint in his studio at nine that night, I felt very pleased with our plan. We had organised our lives and I had promised to keep a safe, professional distance from dangerous men about to go on trial for murder.

An excellent plan.

Wish I'd stuck to it.

FOURTEEN

With Jeremy in London, Amanda found herself in a huge house in the middle of nowhere with absolutely nothing to do. Or nothing she wanted to do anyway. She wasn't a country girl, didn't understand people who walked up hills just to walk down them again. She found the Scottish countryside so beautiful it was boring. She'd once done a driving tour of the Highlands with a friend and after days exclaiming at the rugged changeability of it she craved a loud smoky nightclub so badly she could have screamed. Without Jeremy, the Crinan Canal had nothing to offer Amanda. No pubs within walking distance, no good cafés or bookshops or litter that spoke of nights out. The canal was just that, a canal. Occasionally she saw yachts with families sitting at the lock waiting for the water to rise then fall again, and she really didn't understand why parents would take their children on such trips, spending most of the day waiting for water to rise then fall again.

She didn't tell her mum and dad that Jeremy had headed south. Or her friends, 'cause this was her honeymoon, this house was for her and Jeremy. So she waited, watching the lock outside, trying to understand the point of sailing and weak jacuzzi baths.

On the second morning she woke to the phone ringing. It was her boy, and he was so sorry, but he had to stay with his mum. She was having tests, and was still refusing to see anyone.

'Let me come down!' Amanda said, but he insisted that she

stay and wait for him. 'At least one of us should enjoy the place,' he insisted.

Alone in Crinan, Amanda thought about Jeremy's relationship with his mother. She first discovered there were serious problems between them when they decided to get married and Jeremy was determined not to invite her and even more determined not to discuss her.

'She won't come,' he said. 'There's no point. We just don't see eye to eye.'

He wouldn't elaborate. 'Please, let's not talk about it,' he insisted.

Amanda figured they'd just grown apart or something, and took it upon herself to intervene. One afternoon, when Jeremy was working, she visited his mother without telling him.

The house was a small terrace in Haringey. Its occupant was a thin, worn woman, dressed in pressed trousers and a tight white T-shirt and firm, fitted pink cardigan. She smelt strongly of alcohol and cigarettes. Her gaunt, heavily lined face had settled in a frown. Unnerved by Jeremy's mother's unfriendly appearance, Amanda introduced herself. Jeremy's mum grimaced and then beckoned her in. The interior was jam-packed with antique furniture that suggested wealth a generation or so ago. A barely opened curtain cast a shaft of light on the dust, smoke and grit that shared the air of the crowded room.

Amanda told Mrs Bagshaw that she and Jeremy were getting married.

'We'd be so happy if you could come,' she said, handing her an invitation she'd designed and printed out on the computer especially. 'Will you come?'

Mrs Bagshaw sat down in the corner of the room, lit a cigarette and poured a glass of pure gin. She inhaled energetically, sucking the life out of her Marlborough full strength so hard that its end sizzled and curved. She exhaled less smoke than Amanda expected considering the hefty intake, and said, 'Let me tell you what your fiancé did.'

The cigarette ash clung on as Mrs Bagshaw told Amanda her half of a terrible story.

'I won't be coming,' she said when she'd finished, tapping the two inches of grey into her overflowing ashtray. 'And I'd prefer if you didn't visit me again.'

Amanda didn't even try not to cry on the tube on the way home. She was devastated for Mrs Bagshaw, but even more devastated for her beloved Jeremy. She rushed into their Islington flat and immediately confessed her secret mission, hugging Jeremy tight and telling him how sorry she was, so sorry, please hug me, please hug me, please talk to me.

So Jeremy hugged her, and then told her his half of the story.

As she sat alone by the window in Crinan, Amanda pieced the two stories together in her mind, imagining the terrible events of Jeremy's childhood.

Jeremy's parents met while they were both travelling in New Zealand. They then settled into a very happy affluent life in London. Jeremy's father, Richard, was an accountant. His mum, Anne, had been a lawyer. Before having kids they loved travelling, had friends around as often as they could, held hands, cuddled on the sofa, and slept for at least eight soothing hours a night. They had love and laughter, passion and spark.

When Jeremy came into the world, they lived in a flat near Tower Bridge, just like the one Jeremy and Amanda lived in. On coming home from the hospital with their beautiful baby boy, Richard had filmed him as they escorted him around his new house.

'This is your room, Jer!' Richard said excitedly. 'This is

your panda, and this is your tiny cute little baby-grow thingy, and this is where Mummy will wipe your bottom.'

'Where Daddy will wipe your bottom!' said Anne, and they laughed a lot, as they were prone to do in those days.

The first year was not the hell that Anne had been warned to expect. In fact, it was the happiest year of her life. She took twelve months off and spent a lot of it admiring her son, looking into his eyes and being awed by his cleverness. He was handsome, and very well behaved, and the bond between mother and child was rock solid.

By the time Jeremy was three and a half, they had built the new architect-designed house on the outskirts of Oxford overlooking fields. Jeremy loved running around the huge garden, collecting things like straight sticks and small spiders. He kept them in the clever storage facility under his bed, adding to his collections each day, proudly looking them over and re-organising them so that they made more sense.

One day, when Jeremy was nearly four, he was midway through putting his sticks in order of straightness and then length when his mother came into the room holding something in her arms. It was a baby, his sister, and she was such a good girl, so gorgeous.

'Look at her eyes!' said his mother, unable to take hers away even for one second to look at his new stick system.

Jeremy had vague recollections of his mum before the baby came along. He could picture her making him mashed potato with sausages and tomato ketchup. He could almost hear himself saying 'You're my best girl' and almost see her smiling face as she said 'Yes, my love, I am, and you're my best boy'. He could recall playing hide and seek in the park with her, and reading stories at night. He could picture how interested she always was in the sticks he had collected, and how – at night – she laughed and danced in the kitchen with a bottle of pinot grigio half full on the breakfast bar.

But everything changed after his sister came home.

Bella she was called. She had thick dark hair and a squashed nose and she cried. And cried. And the laughing and dancing in the kitchen turned to yelling and screaming. The park strolls were replaced by frantic drives around and around town until Bella got to sleep.

As for his stick collections, Jeremy distinctly recalled his mother using a voice he'd never heard before when she yelled, 'For God's sake Jeremy, those stupid sticks have brought mud in all over the place!'

When he started crying his mother spoke softly for the first time in a week. 'I am *so* sorry, baby boy. I didn't mean that. I'm just tired. Your little sister keeps me up all night with her hungry tummy and her nappies.'

'Well don't use nappies, then.'

'I have to honey, she pees in them and gets all wet and uncomfortable and that's why she cries. I'm sorry, I'm just very tired because there's no one to help. I do love you, my little boy, you know that, don't you? I love you more than ever, and little Bella doesn't change that. I'm just tired, that's all.'

Jeremy went to bed without a story after that and felt so sorry for his mummy. How could he help? He lay awake for hours thinking about it and when Bella cried her piercing cry in the middle of the night it came to him.

He would dry her nappy and his mummy would not have to wake up at all.

He crept into the nursery and looked into the cot. She was so lovely, this poor little girl, so wet and uncomfortable. And he was her big brother and he would look after her. He would pick her up and kiss her on the forehead and look into her special little eyes and hold her head up like he'd been taught to do, and rock her gently back and forth as he walked down the hall, through the kitchen and into the utility room. And he would kiss her once more and smile so lovingly at her, because she was the only little sister he had, and he would touch her on the nose once she was in the barrel and blow her a kiss and then shut the door and her nappy would soon be dry. Then Mummy and Daddy would have a good night's sleep so that tomorrow they would drink a bottle of pinot grigio and dance and sing in the kitchen.

It was pitch black outside by the time Jeremy figured the nappy would be dry. When he opened the door of the dryer his gorgeous little sister fell out with a thud onto the floor at his feet. It had worked. The nappy was dry as a bone and Bella was quiet as anything, snug and warm without the grimace on her face she always seemed to have. Happy to have helped, he picked her up in his arms and cuddled her gently and kissed her on the forehead and then noticed his mother standing over him in the doorway. His lovely mummy, standing over him, white as a ghost, and then screaming.

And then grabbing his sister from his arms.

And then running to the phone.

And then breathing into Bella's face with her large mouth and not even looking at Daddy who was also white as a ghost.

And then sobbing, sobbing, holding her, little Bella, Mummy and Daddy both crouched over her, rocking and sobbing and screaming 'NOOOO!'.

'Her nappy . . .' Jeremy ventured, as the siren got louder and louder outside, then stopped.

And this is when Jeremy got the look from his mum that he would get from her for the rest his life. Slowly her face withdrew from his lovely little sister and her clenched hands climbed from her thighs to her waist and she stared at him with eyes that were filled with rage and hatred, confused though, because this kind of rage and hatred would usually be followed by action, but this time the eyes just held themselves on him and no action followed.

Ever.

FIFTEEN

Ah fuck, I should've listened to Chas. Not only had I decided to make a completely unnecessary visit to Amanda, but I'd also forgotten to conjure up an imaginary glass cone to protect me from getting emotionally involved. I was welling up. I could hardly see the Ayr Road as I headed back to work from the salon.

Poor Jeremy, I thought.

Wee Bella. I shook my head, a tear falling.

And Jeremy's parent s . . . Imagine.

I stopped the car to compose myself, knowing I needed to get my head together for a meeting with the police.

'Well done,' said Hilary as I came into the office. 'I hear you did well at the pre-release. I'm going to allocate you as Marney's supervising officer.'

'Can I talk to you about that?' I started. I wanted to ask her if I had to supervise paedophiles. I wanted to convince her to give me murderers, drug dealers, car thieves, anyone, rather than child sex offenders.

'Sure,' Hilary said. 'We'll put it on the agenda next supervision. But I'm afraid I have to head home now. Migraine.'

I should probably have given this more thought before applying for the job. These guys were the big yins in criminal justice: high profile, high risk. And very few escaped social work supervision since the new Sex Offenders Act, which meant that our teams were bulging at the seams with rapists, flashers, stalkers, lewd and libbers, etcetera, etcetera. There'd probably be no way of avoiding them, even if I told

Hilary why I felt so uncomfortable. Or did everyone feel this way? Not just those who'd been touched by one in the past? I'd tell her, I decided to myself, at our next supervision session – and ask for her advice.

Looking in the mirror of the grotty office toilet a few minutes later, I was thinking to myself that I looked a bit like Jodie Foster, when someone farted unashamedly in the cubicle, the force of it bringing me back down to earth – Glasgow earth and not Hollywood. Soon after, Penny walked out and said hello and I wondered how she could just smile and wash her hands like that, as if nothing had happened. Not even a slight blush or an apology (I'd have done both if a fart of mine had managed such longevity and volume). I guess her upper-middle-class self felt there was no need, that if one was to fart then one should let rip in the communal toilet. I didn't like Penny.

'How you doing?' I asked her.

'Fine,' she replied. 'Busy busy!'

FARTY! FARTY! I thought as she left, before returning to my pre-gusset-burp line of thinking which was that I looked and indeed was a little bit like Jodie Foster as Clarice Starling – tough and sexy and embedded in a shocking murder case.

I took my place at a risk management meeting that afternoon. It was about James Marney again, the 'lewd and libber' (i.e. a kid-toucher-upper). As I was now his supervising officer – although I would do everything in my power to get Hilary to change her mind – I needed to find him somewhere to live quick smart.

We spent about half an hour sharing soft intelligence. God, even the words used in my job were sexy – soft intelligence, and even better than that, hard intelligence! It was practically as good as my bunny.

'Krissie?' said the police officer, Bond, clicking his fingers at me and stilling my wandering mind. Without even thinking about it, I had placed a cone of silence over my head. All I'd caught was something about needing to check with the housing officer in the prison. 'Can you get onto it and let me know as soon as they have something for us to check out?'

'Of course,' I said, and we exchanged direct telephone numbers.

While my colleagues were tear-arsing around town with a flurry of court reports, absconding sex offenders and homeless drug users, I still only had the one report and one case, so I decided to be thorough.

I rang Jeremy's lawyer, a young man with a lovely English accent. He told me he felt the attacker was probably a known sex offender. There had been several rapes in the Highlands over the last two years, he said, and one sexual assault and murder. The case against Jeremy was weak, he believed, and rested on two things: Jeremy's mother's alibi, and the DNA.

In relation to the alibi, Jeremy's mother was not corroborating her son's story. After being discharged from hospital, she had consistently maintained that she'd gone home alone, without seeing her son. Jeremy, on the other hand, insisted he had driven his mother to her house in Haringey and stayed with her all night on the night of the murder. The lawyer agreed wholeheartedly with Amanda's assertion that Mrs Bagshaw was lying. Her hatred for her son, and her desire to make him disappear, were more important to her than the truth.

As for the DNA, the lawyer explained, traces of Jeremy's genetic material were found under the victim's fingernails.

'Shit,' I said out loud after I hung up. Danny looked at me, having heard the entire conversation.

'Be careful with defence lawyers,' Danny warned. 'You don't want to be used as a plea in mitigation.'

'I know, of course. I just find it really interesting.'

And boy, did I!

70

I was on a roll. First, I phoned the Scottish Criminal Records Office and asked if the list of previous convictions had arrived from England. It had, and when I received the fax I wasn't surprised to find that Jeremy had none.

Next I contacted social services in Oxford and asked if there had been any previous contact. No.

Jeremy had given me authority to talk to his childhood GP, so I phoned Dr Charles McQuillan of John Street in Oxford who said he'd had little contact since it had happened, just the odd ear infection, but psychological and psychiatric reports at the time drew a blank. A bit of bedwetting, but nothing much else. 'Looked like a terrible accident,' Dr McQuillan said.

Then I rang Mrs Anne Bagshaw, Jeremy's mum. The alibi stories were so different. Someone was lying. I wondered if she would talk to me.

'Hello?' I said, and introduced myself, explaining who I was, where I worked, the report I was writing for court, and that the judge wanted to know all about Jeremy's background and any psychological issues that might affect his response to custody. I went on about how I knew it was very difficult for her, but that I'd seen Jeremy and he was coping all right in prison and that he'd said he didn't mind if I called and spoke about –

It was about then I realised she'd put the phone down.

I felt irritated. Why would she put the phone down? No matter what her son did in the past, or had done now, he was still her son, and should surely –

'I think we got cut off,' I said after she picked up the second time, and the phone immediately went dead again.

I was annoyed.

'Don't hang up!'

But she did, and my anger grew each time the phone rang out after that. What was going on? She seemed to have

71

completely cut Jeremy out of her life. What kind of mother would desert her son like that?

Over the next two days, I gained five cases and two reports, which Danny had been entrusted to allocate as Hilary was still off sick.

Danny's allocations meetings consisted of the four of us sitting around Danny's desk with a pile of report requests and orange files in the middle, playing paper, scissors, stone.

I did a bomb (thumb up, beats everything) each time a sex offender appeared, and while Robert and Danny maintained that bombs are not part of the game, Penny told them to let it be.

'Just leave it,' she said. 'I'll take them.'

After the game was completed, we spent a half-hour swapping anyway, using arguments like:

He lives near my house, so I don't want him 'cause I'll keep bumping into him.

He lives near my house, so I do want him so I can do home visits 3.30 each Friday.

I had her last time. Your turn Mrs.

Give me that. I love thugs.

Give me him, the little bastard.

So I gained five cases and two reports, none of them sex offenders.

I also gained a smoking habit.

How could I resist smoking at work? Smokers had the naughty gene. They were the fun guys who sought out danger, and were undeterred by rain or wheezing. The smokers in my office were rowdy, usually hung-over, and knew all the office gossip. During my six or so fag breaks in those first two days as a reformed-reformed smoker, I discovered the following:

– Funny-tall-guy Robert shagged social work assistant Jane at last year's Christmas party. Her love for him lingered, demonstrated by her post-festive-season weight loss, new haircut and broken marriage. Robert insisted it never happened, but two smokers saw it: one in the flesh, and one on a sheet of A4 photocopying paper.

– Charlie from Govan brought gin into work in his satchel.
– Charlie from Govan accused his boss, Jill, of bullying him.
– Charlie from Govan was a wanker.
– So was his boss, and a bully.

Smokers! Ah! What would work be without them? They laughed. They moaned the glorious moan of the social worker. They knew how to get the most out of mileage and overtime claims. And most of all, they had cigarettes. I was at the pre-contemplative stage of smoking, which meant I hadn't yet stood up in a crowd and admitted my addiction. Which also meant I never bought my own.

So my first week came and went, and by the end of it I was a shit-hot parole officer – if a little over-empathetic – a smoker, and almost as neglectful of my son as Mrs Bagshaw had been of hers.

It seemed as if Robbie had grown about ten feet and learnt about a hundred new words when I finished up on the Friday, and when I came in he didn't run to me and hug me and never want to let me go. He looked up at me and then went back to making his magic fairy potion with Chas. So far, they'd put in self-raising flour, water, Nesquik (chocolate *and* banana), oats and honey, and they were now considering what to add next.

'Loganberries!' said Robbie.

He had never said this word before. Indeed, few people I knew had.

'Where did you find out about loganberries?' I asked him, but he couldn't be bothered answering me because he and

73

Chas had decided that the fairies in the drying green would probably prefer bubble bath.

I had no role in Robbie's life any more, I thought, sighing. I was away every day, and he was with other people, learning from them, hanging out with them, changing. As I bathed him later on I realised that there was no such thing as quality time, only quantity time, and he wasn't getting that with me. Just like Jeremy's mother, I'd removed myself from his life.

'Oh shut up!' said Chas after the story and our family cuddle. 'Every mother feels this. It's natural. You're a wonderful mum and Robbie adores you. You're just shattered. It's Friday, so you have two whole days of quantity time ahead of you.'

Chas took off to the studio the next morning and Robbie and I made pancakes and a huge mess. He sat up at the kitchen bench with a tea towel tucked into his 'I'm easily distracted' T-shirt, and broke three eggs against a glass bowl. The first two landed on the floor, but Robbie cracked the last one like a TV chef – a neat bang to the middle with a firm right hand, the left hand moving in for the separation, a quick wrist-flick upwards, and there we had it! A perfect shell-less egg in a bowl. We sang a song to celebrate – something about Donald egg-crackers being the best damn egg-crackers in the world. It was wonderful.

Afterwards, we walked to the park and tossed burnt pancakes to the ducks. After that we went to the transport museum and I watched the Rob-mobile run from tram to bus to bike to car to ye-oldy-streety-with-ye-oldy-undergroundy-stationy. It was a fabulous day with a lot of laughing. At bedtime when I asked Robbie what he'd liked about the day he said 'Everything, Mummy' and hugged me so hard I wanted to weep with joy.

SIXTEEN

Back when he'd had his first interview with Krissie Donald, Jeremy had returned to his cell and been surprised to find that the officer who'd escorted him back didn't lock the door to his cell.

He took to his bunk to think over what he'd spoken to Krissie about – his love for Amanda, how much he missed her, how he could never see her again. The social worker had offered to supervise a visit, if it would make things easier, but he'd refused. He couldn't see Amanda full stop. It was too hard.

While he'd been musing about things, a prisoner had appeared at his cell door, unsupervised. He was scarred, scary and built like a brick shithouse. Jeremy had seen him before – in the quadrangle, and also in Agents. He'd been in the interview room across the way, and he'd stared at Jeremy for a frightening amount of time with Alpha Dog eyes and a small smile on his face.

Jeremy had sat up, his brain throbbing with what might be about to happen. Was the brick shithouse going to rape him? Would Billy hold him down while the brick shithouse pushed his filthy cock into his bottom? Or maybe the other way around, or maybe both.

Looking over the shoulder of the large prisoner, he saw an officer on the landing, but the officer just winked. Oh God, both, plus the guard, all three. Shit, oh shit.

'Billy here knows your little friend,' said the brick shithouse, psychopath grin still there.

'Sorry?' Jeremy said, trying to control his panic.

'Your social worker friend, Krissie Donald.'

'Uh-huh?' Jeremy didn't know what else to say. As it turned out, he hadn't needed to because the script had been written for him.

'Billy worked with her boyfriend in the cook's room a few years back, didn't you Billy?'

Billy didn't answer.

'Billy says there were photos of her all over the guy's cell. He was in love, wasn't he, Billy? Billy's friends with him still, aren't you, Billy?'

Billy still hadn't said anything.

'Oy, Billy, you're mates with her man, aren't you?'

'Aye,' came a mousey response.

'Knows all about him, where he lives, which is where she lives. I think their friendship's about to come in handy.'

Billy watched from his top bunk as the brick shithouse kicked into Jeremy's stomach, head, legs, arms. He didn't move.

Jeremy remembered the feeling of fists pounding into his face, knees, groin. He'd thought he was going to die, and he probably would have if he hadn't said yes.

Yes, he understood that she wouldn't be searched as vigilantly.

Yes, Billy was sure to get out shortly.

Yes, he would get her to bring the stuff in.

Yes, if she didn't, then the next visit wouldn't be so pleasant.

Jeremy looked at Krissie during that second interview and thought about her home situation. She'd already told him she had a son. She'd told him she was in love too, and so she understood how hard it must be for him. It was clear she was kind and naïve, that she was someone with love and hope in her life.

And he couldn't do it, so he left the room.

But afterwards it wasn't only a beating. It was as bad as he could have possibly imagined.

The worst thing wasn't how sore it was being held down, or having the small tub of Flora Light margarine from someone's lunch spread over his white loaf while his mouth was gagged with an old sock; the worst, most awful thing was that halfway through, Jeremy got an erection. When he thought over the twenty-minute ordeal, often waking in a sweat with the memory of it, it was this that made him most angry of all. While being brutally raped by an ugly stinking dangerous man, with a junkie ned looking down from his top bunk, he had somehow gotten himself a hard-on.

SEVENTEEN

When Jeremy walked into the interview room to see me for the third time, something had changed.

'You're looking a bit better,' I lied. He looked freshly bruised, and broken.

'Thanks,' he said, taking his seat cautiously.

I decided not to press him about his bruises. There was no point. He'd talk to someone when he felt ready. Instead, I spent the next twenty minutes doing the 'final interview', which involved reading over what I'd written so far and making alterations where necessary. I hated doing this, but he had a right to hear it. I imagined how I'd feel if someone read their version of my life story to me. Pissed off to the point of head-butting is how I'd feel. But being completely upfront about what I'd written was the right thing to do, so I soldiered on, telling Jeremy to stop me if he had any queries or issues whatsoever.

1. Family details:

Amanda Kelly, wife, nail technician.

Richard Bagshaw, father, accountant (No contact since subject aged 4)

Anne Bagshaw, mother, lawyer (No contact since subject aged 16)

2. Income:

£120,000 per year: Self-employed property developer.

3. Personal circumstances:

Jeremy Bagshaw is an only child. He was raised in Oxford,

England. His parents divorced when he was four years old after a terrible childhood accident, when the subject killed his three-week-old sister by placing her in the dryer to stop her crying. The subject feels this has impacted on his relationship with both parents. His father left the family home shortly afterwards and has had no contact with the subject since. As far as Mr Bagshaw is aware, his father remarried and moved to Canada. Jeremy's mother sent him to boarding school at the age of nine. She saw very little of the subject during his years at boarding school, sending him to camp during the holidays, and had no contact with him after he completed his Highers. Mr Bagshaw understands that his mother finds it very difficult to see him, as it reminds her of the terrible loss that was his fault. He feels immense remorse for what he did.

Psychiatric and psychological reports, provided by Dr McQuillan of Oxford (see attached), state that the subject was bedwetting at the age of four, but displayed none of the other possible precursors to personality disorder, although in the psychiatrist's opinion it would be difficult to make firm conclusions when the subject was so young.

Mr Bagshaw's behaviour and attitude after the age of four do not appear to have caused any concerns. Of very high intelligence, he left boarding school with extremely good results. He then went on to complete a degree in science at Oxford University and then a Masters in Business Administration at the University of London.

The subject worked with PPC Jams after graduating and then set up his own business in property development. His business is successful and employs three people.

Mr Bagshaw has no previous offences, and none outstanding. His physical health is good, and he has no history of mental health problems. The subject drinks moderately, and although he has used cannabis and Ecstasy recreationally has never been addicted to illegal substances. ·

Mr Bagshaw says his wife is currently staying with her parents in Glasgow and works in the Pine Tree Unisex Salon in Newton Mearns. He finds the prospect of visits from her too difficult at present. Should he be found not guilty, he intends to 'take things one day at a time'.I was about to read Jeremy the conclusion – that he was aware a life sentence would be the only option available to the court should he be found guilty, and that in my opinion he would find this sentence very difficult, but that there appeared to be no issues in relation to self harm or suicide – when Jeremy suddenly reached out and slapped my hand and the report down to the table.

'What are you doing?' I asked, suddenly scared, his hand still on mine.

Jeremy looked over my shoulders to see if anyone was looking and leaned in towards me, the terror on his face sending a chill up my spine. His words came out almost in a whisper.

'I'm in danger,' he said.

'What?'

'I'm in danger,' even softer this time.

'What is it?'

But he was crying so hard he was unable to get the words out, and I found myself moving to the other side of the desk without even thinking about professionalism and distance and being seen as a soft touch, and putting my arm around him.

'It's okay, it's okay. Tell me.'

'Please, just go back to your seat. If I tell you it might happen again . . . or worse.'

'Tell me what's happening.'

'I can't, I'm in danger. Krissie, listen to me. We're *both* in danger.'

EIGHTEEN

What the hell did Jeremy mean, we were both in danger? He'd rushed from the interview room after blurting that out, leaving me confused and worried and in desperate need of advice. I drove as fast as I could back to the office, but when I got there Danny was on home visits, Robert was at Shotts Prison, Penny was banging things around on her desk (and in any case was the last person I wanted to talk to), my boss was still off sick, and my boss's boss was in a risk management meeting with his boss and the police.

I hate being new. You spend days pretending to read things people give you, meeting people you immediately forget, wondering how to go about asking for a stapler that works. Throughout my four-storey office building, everyone but the smokers stuck to their sections like rabbits in winter, scampering out to collect every now and again, but otherwise hibernating in their miserable dark holes. Secretaries were really spies disguised, checking on overuse of staplers, amongst other things, and taking notes. Bosses were formidable giants behind closed doors, rarely available, especially at times of crisis. They weren't to be confused with those of us who did the work, who visited the prisons and the hospitals and the houses, and whose names would be in the paper should anything go wrong.

I decided to wait for my boss's boss – allegedly called Peter McDonald – to get out of the meeting, tell him about what Jeremy had said, and then settle on how to proceed.

Anxious and worried at my desk, I dialled reception to

leave a message for him, hoping he'd call me back with the advice and support I urgently needed.

'How did you get this number?' came an accusing voice.

'It's on my phone list as reception.'

'Well, this is the concierge.'

'Oh, okay. You might want to change the phone list.'

'Just cross it off yours.'

'But then other people might do the same.'

'No one has ever phoned this number instead of reception before, only you.'

And so it went on till the woman at the end, obviously from the concierge and not from reception, hung up on me.

I decided to scrounge a fag, walk to reception, and ask them myself.

'Can you let me know as soon as Peter McDonald gets out of the risk management meeting? I need to speak to him urgently.'

'What about?'

'I'd like to speak to him personally.'

'What's your extension?'

'I can't recall, off hand. Something with a 3 and a 1?'

'If you don't know your extension, how can I call you to let you know when he gets out of the risk management meeting?' She recalled my words in deliberate detail, to make a point.

'My name's Krissie Donald. Hilary Sweeney's team. Why don't you look on your list?'

'Because I'm very busy.'

As I waited back at my desk, Danny's phone rang and I answered it. I learned from what happened next that this was a big mistake. Social workers should never answer each other's phones.

It was one of Danny's probationers, a fifty-something drinker called Chris Campbell, who began by saying he wanted to apologise for missing his anger management class.

'He better not breach me, 'cause I've rang and all, no?'

'Why did you miss it?' I asked.

'Some bastard eye-balled me down the Green.'

'You got into a fight?'

'He eye-balled me.'

'Okay, I'm just writing out your message for Danny . . . "Chris Campbell rang to say he missed his anger management class 'cause he was busy fighting down Glasgow Green".'

He yelled at me for a while – social workers are all the fuckin' same and all cunts, etc. – and as he ranted, my phone rang. I couldn't get him off the line to answer it because he stated crying. *He* was the cunt, wasn't he? A cunt and a waste of space and maybe he should just end it all?

Eventually, my phone having rung out three times, I promised to rewrite the message slightly: 'Danny – Chris Campbell rang. Says he's having a tough time and will come in first thing tomorrow.'

I immediately dialled reception to be informed that my boss's boss and his boss had finished their meeting and left the building.

Shit.

'I asked you not to let that happen!' I said, having raced back down to reception.

'I rang your number three times. It's 3153, by the way,' she said.

In the old days, before I embraced the maturity and wisdom that came with motherhood and true love, I would have taken the bitch by the scruff of her neck and shaken her, or at least said something cutting and witty about her weight. But I had grown, even with a murderer from the most dangerous prison in Europe trusting me with secrets he shouldn't, and instead I said, 'That's right, you did,' and took a seat beside her at reception to wait for the boss's boss to return.

I waited in reception for two hours beside the reception-ist, who fiddled awkwardly with her pens as I breathed heav-ily down her neck. Occasionally she answered the phone, and was incredibly friendly to everyone. She made a point of making points.

Social workers rushed in and out on child protection inves-tigations, grabbing children's car seats from a row piled up opposite the photocopier. Women and men yelled in inter-view rooms – at each other, at their workers. Receptionists answered phones and talked about the weekend. Meanwhile, I waited.

And waited.

But the boss's boss and his boss did not return and before long I was alone in the locked office, and when I left it was getting dark and someone had scratched 'Fuck You' on the bonnet of my new bright red Toyota Yaris.

I had to go home. I needed to talk to Chas. He would make me feel better, tell me how to handle things, give me a hug.

'Where the hell have you been?' He accosted me before I had a chance to de-tobacco in the bathroom.

'Hello to you too.'

'I said I needed to be at the studio for seven!'

'Oh God!' I couldn't believe I'd forgotten. Chas only had a few days to get things ready for his exhibition, and every-thing was riding on it.

'Is this how it's going to be? Robbie's asleep. You haven't seen him since eight o'clock and you come in here twelve hours later without even apologising!'

He put on his coat as we began Fight Two.

'Sorry, Chas, you need to listen to me. I've had the worst day –'

But he was already out the door, the keys to the studio in his hand.

He'd be gone as long as it took, painting whatever the fuck he painted until he felt calm again.

And so I was alone with my problem. I peeped into the nursery where Robbie was sleeping with his bum up in the air. His perfect mouth was slightly opened and resting on the pillow and his huge eyelashes curled up towards his eyebrows. My boy.

After throwing yet another pizza in the bin, I remembered my pre-pregnancy stash of fags. They were hidden in a plastic container above a wall unit in the kitchen. I smoked all seven of them in a row, stale and revolting as they were, and then lay awake all night, drifting in and out and wondering if I'd been drifting in and out, or simply been awake all night. Chas didn't come home.

I was cranky and irritable with Robbie the next morning. Obsessed with gathering toys to take to nursery to set up a shop, he filled his Thomas suitcase with God knows what. He wouldn't eat his porridge, and refused to stay still as I put his clothes on and brushed his teeth. I raced around after him at a hundred miles an hour, my voice taking on an evil-witch-from-hell tone as I got more exhausted with each lap of the flat.

For the first and last time ever, I smacked him. On his hand. He stopped still and looked at me with eyes that were disappointed and betrayed while he prepared for the cry of a lifetime.

So when I dropped him off at nursery, I not only felt awful for condemning him to spend the day with young nursery nurses who didn't love him, but I also felt awful because I'd just smacked my darling defenceless three-year-old.

NINETEEN

Jeremy had berated himself after he'd left the interview with Krissie the day before. How could he have done what he just did? Worried Krissie like that by telling her she was in danger? He liked her. She was honest, non-judgemental. And he hadn't meant to worry her.

It was the last straw, so before he got back to his cell he asked to make some phone calls.

He hadn't heard Amanda's voice since he saw her after the arrest, in a brown brick station in Glasgow. The time before that was better. He'd waved goodbye at the house in Crinan, both of them tearful because they didn't want to be apart, but filled to the brim with love and happiness. Yet here he was on a blackened phone in a Victorian prison hearing her voice again. 'Goodbye, Amanda,' he said, as he drank her in. 'I just want to say goodbye.'

The next call was harder for him.

'I'm sorry,' he told his mum when she finally answered. 'I'm just ringing to say I'm sorry, for the past, and now.'

Initially, Anne Bagshaw hadn't moved as the phone rang over and over again, messages filling the answer phone with weepy desperate beggings:

'Please talk to me, please forgive me.'

'Mum? Please pick up . . . It's Jeremy. I didn't mean it.'

'I deserve to be punished, and I want to be, but I want you to know how much I love you.'

'I want you to know I didn't mean to ruin your life.'

'Please pick up, let me hear your voice before I leave, you have to hear me say how sorry I am. I've been speaking to

this social worker, this best girl called Krissie, and she's helping me. I know what to do. Even from in here I can move
on. I can sort things.'

Stunned and mortified, Jeremy's mum put down her glass
of gin when she heard her son's last message. Picking up the
phone, she listened to her son speak and her eyes changed
for the first time in twenty-four years, the ice dripping round
the edges.

'I'm sorry,' Jeremy said. 'I'm just ringing to say I'm sorry.'
They were both silent for a moment.

'Amanda would be better off without me.'

'Jeremy?' said his mother. 'Are you okay?'

But he'd hung up, gone. She stared ahead, knowing that
she could no longer lock him away. The time had come to
see him, talk to him, perhaps even forgive him.

A few moments later, Anne Bagshaw booked a flight to
Glasgow.

A few moments after that, while heading back to his cell,
Jeremy plopped himself over the metal rail of the second-
floor landing.

He woke up some time later with his nose through the hard
wire and several officers and nurses beneath him.

They got a stretcher onto the wire and placed him on it,
and he wasn't sure if he wasn't moving because he couldn't
or because they'd told him not to. The prison jiggled as he
was carried – all ceilings and lights and worried faces – and
stopped when he got to the health centre, a stone building in
between his hall and the social work unit. The next thing he
knew there were five people around him filling in booklets.

'You know, if you'd really wanted to do it, mate, you'd
have jumped from the top.'

He'd only jumped from the second-floor landing, one
storey to the net. Which was why he was sore, but barely
injured.

They barraged him with questions that were accusations really:

Do you feel like killing yourself?
Have you tried to kill yourself before?
Have you ever scratched yourself?
What are those marks on your chest?

Jesus, Jeremy thought to himself as the booklets were filled in. You're even punished for wanting to kill yourself in prison – don't do this, don't do that, you silly boy, you useless idiot, you'll be watched for this, four times an hour.

Eventually the uniforms left to confer with each other, and Jeremy and I were alone in a cell that was not a suicide cell, and which therefore had sheets, wooden bunks and all the usual trimmings.

TWENTY

On the way to work I actively entered the contemplative stage of smoking, whereby the smoker admits their addiction by actually purchasing a packet of their own. It was a necessary step, as my thus-far-fun smoking colleagues had started saying things like 'I only have two left' and 'I've just been out'.

Before I made it to my desk the next morning, the receptionist handed me a telephone message that read: 'Call Amanda. It's urgent.'

'Jeremy tried to kill himself yesterday,' Amanda said when I phoned her from the duty room in the main reception area. 'Can you get me in to see him?'

After making several calls, I collected Amanda from her home and drove to Sandhill.

There'd been six suicides in Sandhill in as many months, very bad PR, and drastic steps were being taken to avoid further overriding the performance target of three suicides a year. Hence the governor allowed us to go into the 'sui' cell. Amanda was the first relative allowed inside since a mother came in during a hostage situation in '98 and told her son to 'give that girl back NOW!'. (It worked.)

It was the same size and shape as the others – six by eight, cream-painted bricks with some kind of wood chip sprinkled through, arched at the top, but with absolutely nothing in it except a large clock that ticked and ticked and ticked and if you didn't really want to kill yourself before going in there, you sure as hell did after.

Tick Tick Tick Tick. That's all the two of us heard as we

stood at the door of the concrete cell. Jeremy was huddled in the corner. He was absolutely still, his face covered with his arms. He seemed tiny.

Amanda looked scared. She didn't recognise him, and didn't know what to do. I pushed her arm gently towards him, and she moved into his corner of the ring.

She crouched down slowly. He didn't move. She knelt on the floor. She slowly pressed her head into his neck, and nuzzled, and he groaned. She flung her arms around him, enveloped him, and the two of them fell messily into a pile on the floor, clinging to each other, unable to get close enough, howling.

'I can't look at you,' Jeremy said. 'I've ruined your life. I ruin things.'

'You haven't ruined anything,' Amanda told him. 'You've made my life worth living, and we'll get through this.'

I was on the verge of tears as I watched them – her trying to get eye contact, him too distraught to give it – and I wanted to leave their intimacy well alone, leave that space. But I wasn't allowed, and so I stayed as Amanda talked to him. He couldn't leave her. She needed him. The trial hadn't even started yet. He'd get off. They'd still be okay. They'd have their honeymoon. He wasn't to go anywhere, not without her, not without her.

After forty minutes or so, Amanda was asked to leave and I sat with him for a while.

'You're going to survive this,' I said. 'You have to. You see how much she loves you?'

'I didn't kill that woman. But I killed my baby sister. I deserve everything I get.'

'You have to forgive yourself,' I said, knowing that he would never be able to deal with the present unless he confronted his past.

'But how?' he asked.

I was stumped. How does someone forgive themself?

Did he need to be forgiven by someone else first?

By his dad, who'd fucked off to Canada to a dot.com family not long after Bella died?

His mum, who refused to see him or even talk to him and who was probably lying to police to keep him locked away, out of sight?

Stuck for suggestions, I found myself asking, 'Are you religious?'

'I was baptised Catholic, but after the funeral we stopped going to Mass.'

'Maybe you should see the Chaplain,' I blurted, and this from me – the worst Catholic in the world – who'd once stolen twenty pence from the collection plate, crossed my arms tight through the sermon and pinched Geoffrey McTavish's arms till he cried, who'd regularly made up stories as a teenager (*Forgive me father for I touched Shane O'Dowd's penis behind the tennis shed . . .*) just to hear Father O'Hair choke in his little box.

'I'll organise it for you,' I said.

I left Jeremy in his horrible sui cell and went over to Agents to see James Marney.

'I'm going to be your supervising officer,' I said, trying hard to ignore the queasy feeling in my stomach.

Okay, so part of my job was to protect his children, and I'd done well in this regard so far. But – until I could talk to Hilary – another part was to help him be law-abiding. To do this I needed to get to know the man beyond the crime. I put my past as far to the back of my mind as I could and continued.

'The parole board have asked me to identify another place for you to live. As long as this is suitable, your expected date of release won't change. I'll be working with the police and with the child protection team to find you a flat. When you get out, I'll be visiting you regularly and working with you to help you avoid offending. It's best if we can be upfront. So you need to be honest with me. Child protection will be assessing the situation with your children. If they feel your parents can't protect them, further steps may be taken to ensure their safety. We need to work together on this.'

He'd obviously decided on a different tack since the pre-release case conference. He stared at me, through me, and was steadfastly silent. As I looked into his eyes, I tried not to see him watching hardcore porn and asking his sons to touch his penis; I tried not to see Sarah's stepfather locking the en-suite door, not to hear Sarah knocking and crying from inside it as I did as I was told.

'James?' I prodded, but he wouldn't answer. He hated my guts.

Despite my efforts, the feeling was mutual.

I suggested he should go back to his cell and think over if he wanted to get out at all, and then headed over to the social work unit. Situated in a separate building in the middle of the prison and looking like a run-down country cottage, the social work unit was filled with chatty admin staff and an eccentric mixture of oddball social workers who seemed to do nothing unashamedly for very long periods of time.

After being offered biscuits and chocolates by the friendly receptionist, I caught up with the prison housing officer, who'd located a one-bedroom council flat for the lovely James Marney. Police would check it out and let me know if it was suitable. I then asked to see Bob, the prison social worker who'd been at the pre-release meeting. His office was in the eaves of the building. Classical music was playing from the radio, a large shop-like display of food was carefully arranged on a table in the corner, and Bob was having a power nap at his desk. He woke to the sound of the door shutting – 'Good morning, Miss Donald!' he said – and offered me one of the Turkish delights he'd bought during his fortnight in Istanbul-not-Constantinople, then issued me with an invitation to the next work-book-club at the Beer Café. Bob told me that Jeremy Bagshaw had returned from his interview with me at Agents, made some phone calls, then jumped off the second-floor landing of the remand hall. He wasn't hurt badly because the net caught him at first-floor level, Bob told me, but when they'd left him alone in the health centre for five minutes he'd tied the sleeves of his shirt around his neck, ripped the body of his shirt and tied it to the leg of the bed, then spent the next four minutes trying to strangle himself because there was no height for hanging. He'd maintained a long, determined pull against the leg of the bed – pull, pull, head away from the bed, away, until the air was less and then nothing. I wondered how anyone could do this. I understood jumping off a building or kicking a chair, when one quick and irreversible movement it all it takes, no turning back. But maintaining the effort through-out, when you could change your mind and just stop, just live, seemed incredible.

It hadn't been a success, Bob said, because the uniforms in the health centre corridor had put their booklets down and turned around for a Code Blue.

Bob finished a game of mini-basketball (he had a net set up on his office door) and then escorted me to the Chaplaincy.

Father Moscardini was a good-looking Scots-Italian man of about forty. His clothes were well ironed and he was trim and smiley. His wee room contained loads of cookery books and biographies. The radio was on. Father Moscardini was nothing like Father O'Hair or any of the other unhappy-looking priests I'd met as a child. He loved his job, and found giving comfort to men who were often at their lowest very rewarding. He'd just come back from performing a wedding for one of the inmates.

'They seemed very much in love,' the priest said. 'It was very moving.'

94

'I want to talk to you about Jeremy Bagshaw,' I said, explaining his situation and his tragic past. 'He's worried about opening up.'

'He needn't be worried,' Father Moscardini said. 'I'll go over and see him this afternoon.'

TWENTY-ONE

Something weird was happening to me. It started innocently enough, as an interview disguised as a manicure, but it was snowballing into other girly pursuits such as buying perfume and browsing in wedding dress boutiques that I'd accidentally parked in front of.

'When's the big day?' the assistant at Giuseppina Botti asked me.

I replied that I hadn't set a date yet. Even if I had, I would probably buy a reasonably priced trouser suit that I could wear again to various occasions and was I still talking out loud? If I was, the assistant wasn't listening; she was checking my sizes.

I had only ever worn a dress once, and it hadn't been pleasant. I'd spent the whole evening with a scowl on my face hoping to God I didn't have to run for a fire exit. Dresses were nonsensical, and yet the white gloriousness I was trying on was making me flush. Touching the raw silk of one in particular seemed to bring on the swelling sensation I had recently come to understand.

I tried on several, but in the end it was the V-neck mermaid sheath with vertical passimentarie detail and floral-embroidered bust that spoke to me so loudly I paid £1,320 for it, on Visa. I'd return it, no doubt, but I couldn't resist taking it home with me, even if just for a few days.

Why did I do that? Something very strange was happening to me. Maybe it was the Chaplain who'd reminded me of the world of ritual I'd forsaken, or the tragic newly-weds, or moving in with Chas, or maybe it was Robbie, who was sleeping much better, and life was getting easy again, and I wouldn't want that, would I?

I snuck in the front door, got changed into my dress, crept into the spotless living room and went 'Boo!'. Chas and Robbie were hugging on the sofa watching the Tweenies. Robbie lunged at me with his Nutella on toast and covered the whole of the vertical passimentarie detail in chocolate spread.

'Shite!' I said.

'Shite!' Robbie said.

Chas stood nervously at the bathroom door as I banged at the bodice with a wet flannel. It would have been very helpful for Chas at this point if there'd been a little guy at the bottom right-hand side of me 'interpreting for the male'.

CHAS: Are we getting married?

ME: No, I'm just going a bit mad and this dress spoke to me and now it's ruined and I can't take it back!

LITTLE GUY INTERPRETING FOR THE MALE: No, because you haven't asked me, bastard.

CHAS: I thought we didn't believe in marriage.

ME: We don't.

LITTLE GUY INTERPRETING FOR THE MALE: What's not to believe in, prick?

CHAS: Robbie made a shop at nursery today!

ME: Really?

LITTLE GUY INTERPRETING FOR THE MALE: Really? You've changed the subject already? That's it? That's all you have to say when I'm standing here in a stunning wedding dress that's covered in Nutella and my hair's all frizzy and my mascara has smudged and I'm a mad spinster lady. I'm Miss Havish (snort) sham!

Chas grabbed my hand and escorted me into the living room.

'Tell Mummy how much money you made, little one!' Chas said to Robbie.

97

'I made Miss Watson fall over!' Robbie said.

'You didn't check what he packed,' said Chas, relaying what happened after I'd dropped Robbie at nursery that morning.

Robbie had waved me goodbye, touched the window as he always did, then run to the yellow room. His friends Mark Campbell and Evie Brock were setting up shop at the large plastic counter. The children bought, sold, pinged the till and filled their trolleys with glee until Miss Watson came in to make the play more structured and noticed that the only thing left to buy was an Anal Probe.

Little Evie had bought the Twelve Inch Black Dildo, the Nipple Stimulator with Chilli Sex Gel, the Turbo Tongue, and the Slide and Ride. Mark Campbell had bought the Cone, the Three Way Rabbit, the Lusty Licker and the Small Thai Beads. He was laughing like mad because the crotch-less edible underwear was vibrating on top of the eggs that had turned themselves on at the bottom of his blue plastic trolley.

'Buzzy things!' Robbie said, smiling widely as I gazed inside his sex-toy-crammed Thomas the Tank Engine suitcase.

'Oh God,' I said to Chas. 'I am the worst mother in the world.'

TWENTY-TWO

Jeremy had never been a religious man. His mother hadn't encouraged any kind of faith. She'd sent him off to a non-denominational boarding school as soon as she could, leaving him to seek comfort in success, rather than in God. But after Krissie spoke to him about forgiveness, Jeremy realised he wanted and needed the non-judgemental confidence of another.

So Father Moscardini visited Jeremy every day after the terrible low that had caused him to try and squeeze the air from his own lungs. He sat in the interview room in the hall and listened as Jeremy talked about seemingly irrelevant things, like his work, music and cookery. The priest was a sensible, kind man, and he didn't freak Jeremy out with Bible talk.

Neither did he rush him.

'When you're ready, we can talk about the harder things,' Father Moscardini said. 'There's no hurry.'

At the same time each day, Jeremy spent an hour talking about 'easier things', like falling in love with Amanda, feeling safer and calmer each time. After a while, Jeremy began to realise he wasn't alone, he wasn't evil, and he wasn't unworthy. He was a man, and a man could be forgiven.

A few hours after the seventh daily visit from Father Moscardini, Jeremy rang the buzzer beside the door of his cell and asked to be escorted to the chapel.

It took a while, but eventually an officer came and let Jeremy out of his cell.

'You have as long as you need,' the officer said. 'Father Moscardini's okayed it with the hall supervisor.'

The officer led him past B hall and opened a bare metal door beside the segregation unit. Inside, a long concrete hallway led to another nondescript metal door. The officer opened it.

Jeremy was shocked when he saw the chapel. The huge cavernous space had been so well camouflaged and was completely at odds with every other building in the prison compound. A feeling of welcome overcame him as he took in the vast and beautiful place of communal worship.

Seeing the small confessional booth in the corner of the church, Jeremy walked towards it, took a deep breath and opened the door.

'Are you there?' Father Moscardini said from the darkness. 'There's nothing to be afraid of. It's safe in here. Nothing you say will ever be repeated.'

'Father, is it bad to love someone with everything you have?' began Jeremy.

'It's wonderful. Love is the most wonderful gift we have. It's bottomless.'

'But it hurts.'

'Would you like to talk about your sister, Jeremy?'

Silence.

'Jeremy? Are you there?'

He wasn't. It was too hard. He thought he could, but he couldn't. The very word 'sister' had made him want to vomit.

'Take me back,' Jeremy said to the officer after stepping out of the confessional booth. 'Just get me back to my cell.'

TWENTY-THREE

The period after moving back to the flat and getting myself a full-time job had been hard.

For the previous two years, Mum and Dad had done all of the work of making sure sleep was had, food was eaten, and clothes were cleaned and ironed. Of course, Chas and I had helped with housework and contributed to bills, but during that time I hadn't needed to get a job, and could devote all my energy to Robbie, Chas – and me. Meanwhile, Chas had been able to procrastinate with his painting. All in all, we'd been cocooned from the hard reality of day-to-day life.

But now there seemed to be no time to relax and enjoy each other. Mornings were a frantic race to make breakfast, get clothes on everyone and pack lunches. The evenings often felt as if a whole other day of work needed to be squeezed in – cooking, bathing, washing, tidying, getting Robbie to sleep.

We often slept badly, too. I seemed to have inherited Mum's fidgety feet. Chas snored. And Robbie invariably crawled in between us in the early hours, wriggling and pushing at us till Chas and I were perched at each edges of the bed.

Then we finally woke to the alarm and the whole process began all over again.

Weekends didn't seem to be much better. Most of Saturday was spent recovering from work, while Sunday involved a fair bit of dreading the week ahead.

No matter how hard we tried, neither of us was able to leave our work in our respective workplaces. Jeremy was on my mind constantly, as were several other distressing cases I'd been allocated. And Chas was always off in a dwam, his face blank and distant as he thought about what stroke, what colour, what frame he might use for a painting. His opening wasn't far away, and I could tell he was terrified.

Sometimes I wondered if it would have been different for me and Chas if we'd been together before I had the baby. At least then we'd have had some 'us' time. As it was, Chas and I got together when Robbie was nine months old. Chas loved him with all his heart, but Robbie wasn't his baby, and our relationship had been plunged into a very domestic routine, with little time for us to get to know each other as people, and not just as parents.

But the thing about us, the thing that separated us from so many of my other friends who'd had affairs, or withheld sex and affection, or split up, or just whined on and on about each other, was that we talked.

The Nutella rinsing out in the bath, Chas and I went over our mistakes, which included:

Me expecting a tidy house when a tidy house was indicative of nothing more than tidiness.

Chas working all night every night towards his exhibition, being preoccupied and nervous about it, and worrying all the time about whether he would ever be able to provide for us.

Me getting too close to a client and needing advice at work but not getting it.

Chas feeling left out of the whole orgasm thing and wondering if there was something wrong with him.

Me thinking I was a bad mother because I didn't look after Robbie 24/7.

Once again, we made some plans:

Nine to five was a rule, for both Chas and me. No late nights, no excuses. Family time was sacrosanct.

I had to talk to my colleagues more if my bosses were never there.

Chas had to stop beating himself up re my orgasms being machine-induced.

I had to stop beating myself up about Robbie, who loved the nursery in the mornings, and spent the rest of the time with people who adored him.

Chas had to switch off worrying about his painting when he wasn't at the studio.

I had to find a bloody cleaner!

I had to leave off about marriage for a while. We'd only just moved in together and we needed to take one step at a time.

Spooning in bed, we felt confident that work and domestic difficulties would never get the better of us again.

TWENTY-FOUR

There were ten cases and three court reports in my pigeon-hole the next morning. My boss – newly returned to work – had also left a note saying she would be out of the office attending a training course. I had to laugh when I saw the course was called, of all things 'Absentee Management: everything you need to know about dealing with and reducing staff absences'. 'Any questions, ask Eileen', the note concluded.

I had no idea who Eileen was but could be fairly certain she would either be off sick, in a meeting or doing a training course, or have a queue of hyperventilating child protection workers waiting at her door.

I had the usual fag and gossip, listened to Robert sing a song he'd written about a famous glamour model, and leafed through my new cases.

The first was a fifty-year-old lifer. Back when he was twenty, he'd shaken his baby to death, his defence being that his girlfriend should never have left him to look after the screaming wean all the time. He'd done ten years, and then been recalled to prison three times since his initial release for drink-related offences – drink-driving, assault and breach of the peace.

'Ah, that one used to be mine,' said Danny. 'I asked Hilary not to give it to me again 'cause his couch is so sticky.'

'Cheers, Dan,' I said, skimming two other cases: an elderly Asian woman who'd bought £13,000 worth of marble for her kitchen, hall, bathroom, en-suite and living room using other people's credit cards; and a seventeen-year-old girl who'd deliberately set her house on fire ("cause she was in a bad mood'), leaving her cousin chronically ill and seriously disfigured.

I'd just finished the sending out of a batch of letters introducing myself and asking people to come into the office when the phone rang. It was Jeremy's mother, Mrs Bagshaw. And she was in Glasgow.

I arrived at the Clyde View Self-Catering Apartments half an hour later. Mrs Bagshaw was in number 12, a modern flat in a glass building overlooking the murky Clyde.

'What a view!' I said, in an attempt to endear myself to her.

It took a cup of tea and several minutes before our conversation turned to the more pressing topics of murder and suicide.

Anne Bagshaw was a cold, intense woman with a tight, unlovable face. She was over-ironed, smelt of gin, and asked about her son in what felt to me like a very odd way, wanting to know about the details of the offence he'd been imprisoned for and the nature of his injuries. 'Was he hit on the forehead?' she asked when I told her he'd been beaten.

I could understand that Anne Bagshaw had difficulty talking about her son. Her life had been torn apart by Bella's death, and its circumstances must have haunted her constantly.

But shouldn't she feel for her son as well? I'd been wondering how I'd feel about Robbie if he did something dreadful as a toddler, and believed that I would feel terrible for him, love him more and do everything I could to protect him from the guilt and pain of what had happened. But then it hadn't happened to me.

The past aside, Anne Bagshaw's lack of concern for Jeremy's current situation surprised me. Why was she asking such bizarre questions? What did it matter? Her son, her little boy, whom she had loved with all her heart when he was wee, whom she'd breastfed and pushed on a swing, was on remand for murder. He hadn't been found guilty yet. He'd been beaten and perhaps raped. And he wanted to kill himself.

'You must love him very much,' I said, accusing her of the very opposite with my tone.

'No,' she said flatly. 'And it's very hard when you don't love your child. It's hard because you feel guilty. Hard because the child will never go away. Hard, in my case, because I have a very good reason to not love him. Bella never got to have a birthday because of him, my little Bella . . . I have it in mind to surprise him,' she said, snapping-to suddenly.

That was another odd thing. She wanted to surprise him. She'd come all the way from London – I assumed she was intending to corroborate his alibi – but she couldn't quite face seeing him yet and made me promise not to tell him.

By the time I left I was thoroughly bamboozled by everything about her, from the way she looked into my eyes intensely as if she was trying to read my soul, to her inability to forgive her son, to her refusal to see him. I hated that she hadn't got a taxi straight to Sandhill and run to him saying, 'It's okay, it's okay, I'm here!'

When I got back to work I looked at Jeremy's report. I'd practically finished it. As required, I hadn't discussed the offence or meshed my assessment of Jeremy with the crime he was accused of. But as I sat there thinking about Jeremy, his wife and his mother, I became overwhelmed with curiosity about Bridget McGivern, the woman Jeremy was accused of killing. I googled her name: Bridget McGivern.

Several snippets caught my eye:

1. Obituary, *Glasgow Herald*:

Aged 45, beloved mother of Rachel, 18, husband of Hamish, sorely missed, etc., etc.

2. Article, *Daily Record*:

DERMATOLOGIST SLAIN BY PSYCHO SON-IN-LAW

A man was arrested today for the murder of his mother-in-law. The evil Londoner has been charged with the brutal murder of BRIDGET McGIVERN in Crinan, Argyll. The victim, a dermatologist in Stirling, had just reunited with the daughter she gave up for adoption when she was 17. Sources reveal that the accused had a history of violence.

3. Article, *The Scotsman*:

FAMILIES FOR CHILDREN REVIEW

A review into the procedures for reuniting adopted children with their biological parents is under way following the murder of Bridget McGivern. The 45-year-old was killed just two weeks after being reunited with the daughter she gave up for adoption when she was 17. The incident has raised questions about whether our adoption agencies are offering sufficient counselling and support for what is a momentous and life-changing decision. In this case, counselling and support might have averted a terrible tragedy.

As I read about the crime, I realised how terrible and how wrong I'd been to forget about the victim, to push her to one side as if she wasn't relevant. No matter what my job was, this was unforgivable. I'd become so involved with Jeremy

Bagshaw that I hadn't even thought about poor Bridget McGivern.

Bridget McGivern, who'd been married. Who'd left behind an eighteen-year-old daughter. Who'd been a successful dermatologist . . .

. . . and who'd died just two weeks after meeting her long-lost daughter for the first time.

TWENTY-FIVE

Amanda Kelly met Bridget McGivern for the first time in a large dining kitchen in Ballon, Stirlingshire.

Well, that wasn't *really* the first time. The first time they met was twenty-eight years earlier, in a little white hospital room in London with a silver bed and a thin mattress and a metal bench on which there were various contraptions to do with childbirth.

Before Bridget met her untimely death, she'd dreamt about this room often. There'd been paint peeling from one of the walls and a pair of shoes in the corner with blood splattered all over them. There'd been a cheap wee radio beside the metal bench with music so gentle and so soft she'd wanted to hurl it out the window.

There'd also been three people with her: a thin midwife with smoker's skin and breasts a smidgeon higher than is humanly possible; a trainee midwife of twenty or so who seemed more concerned with the perky-bosomed smoker than the prospect of being in charge of the placenta. And then there'd been Bridget's mum, Margaret, who wasn't at all happy that her genius girl was lying back with her fine legs spread wide apart, making no noise. Her daughter, only seventeen, who'd skipped two grades she was so bright and had already started medicine.

Margaret Garden, who was forty at the time, had big plans for her daughter, none of which involved the early production of children. She'd been planning a wonderful graduation party for Bridget, had looked forward to showing her off in the old neighbourhood where none of her friends' children had achieved anything beyond nursing school or, in one case, three-quarters of a wishy-washy arts degree. Margaret had no intention of letting all her plans go to pot because Bridget had had sex with some boy called Hamish in Stirling, who hadn't even finished school yet.

If only she'd kept Bridget at home, she berated herself, not sent her off to halls in London, then she'd have realised in time. God, her friends would gloat if they knew about this baby, especially the ones who'd been aghast at her allowing Bridget to live on campus so far away. 'Bridget's such a sensible girl,' she'd told them back then. And it was true she'd never had any trouble with Bridget; she wasn't like other teenagers who smoked Marlboro Lights down at the bus stop and spent their time speaking to boys or sometimes kissing boys on the lips in the lane behind Croftwood High School.

If only Bridget had taken her advice about sex: don't use condoms, don't use the pill, don't use anything, just don't do it. It's unhealthy, it's overrated and it will hold you back.

If only she'd known sooner, this would never have happened. But Bridget hadn't come home for Christmas, had made excuses at Easter, and by the time Margaret travelled to London to surprise her beloved daughter with two day-passes to the Haymill Baths she was almost in labour.

'Jesus!' Margaret screamed at her daughter as she burst into the grotty shared student living room. 'Jesus, Jesus, Jesus!'

After that she'd fanned herself and sat on the edge of a chair saying Jesus a lot more.

The next day she sprang into action, and before Bridget knew what was happening she'd signed away her baby.

Bridget remembered the face of her mother in that white room – overseeing the procedure, there to the end, ensuring

that the post-birth cuddle wasn't long enough to allow inde-
cision.

She remembered the feeling of relief when the baby
plopped into the midwife's arms, and the feeling of need
when the nurse soothed her crying baby –a little girl who
howled so loudly it scared Bridget.

Bridget had held her, and the baby's howl had turned to a
kind of whimper. Like a sexual noise, almost. Ecstasy. Relief.
Release.

The baby's mouth distorted sideways, reaching for something, and suddenly Bridget understood she needed to lift her
T-shirt and make herself available for the reaching. The little
mouth reached her nipple and the distorted lips honed in,
eyes closed, knowing somehow exactly where to go. Bridget
was overcome with joy, melted by it. She needed to touch
this person, hold her, stroke her arms and legs and tummy
and kiss her forehead and her ears and her little perfect
hands and look endlessly into those eyes, those beautiful
eyes.

'That's it!' said her mother, and the baby was taken away,
its high-pitched cries reverberating down the corridor.

And Bridget was left on the white bed with her T-shirt up,
and her right breast exposed, and her legs open. 'How Deep
is your Love' dripped from the radio while a trembling student nurse pulled what looked like a large lump of liver from
between her legs before slapping it onto the metal bench
under the window.

So that was really the first time they met, Bridget and
Amanda. And while it was heart-wrenching and tragic and
disturbing and unforgettable, it was nothing compared to the
second time.

TWENTY-SIX

I wonder, looking back, if I could have walked away at that point. Not seen Amanda again. Not asked questions about her biological mother, the late Bridget McGivern. Not visited Jeremy.

Would I have walked away if Billy Mullen hadn't turned up on my doorstep just before the trial? Billy Mullen who, I later discovered, had been Jeremy's cell-mate. Billy Mullen, who had also worked with Chas in Sandhill Prison's Cook Room years earlier.

Just twenty-five and a weedy wee gobshite, Billy wore bad-taste designer clothes that cemented his status as a Glasgow ned. Even more so with the scars, one on his right cheek as per the Sandhill uniform, and one on his upper right thigh, which he took every opportunity to show people, even though it involved the removal of his jeans and even though it was still infected from where the 'cunt got me with a machete'.

Billy Mullen knocked on my door at 8 p.m. one evening just after I'd gotten home from a day spent visiting several new probation clients, starting several social enquiry reports, and adding information to Jeremy's report, giving an account of his attempted suicide and noting that he still had the loving support of his wife. After looking up Jeremy's alleged victim on the internet, I had printed and signed the pre-trial report, put it in an envelope and laid it on my desk. Throughout the day I found myself tapping it with my fingers, knowing I should put it in the post, also knowing I was unable to.

'Is the big fella in?' asked Billy when I answered the door.

'Sorry?' I asked.

'The big fella?'

'*Who?*'

'Are you Krissie?'

'Why do you want to know?' I said.

The asking suddenly switched off and the charm switched on. Glasgow banter – the 'ochs' and 'you knows' and 'wee pals' and 'way backs' and 'them rockets from E hall' – all rhythmic and indecipherable, like rap. I gathered, after a while, that he'd known Chas from his stint in prison.

I was just about to deny the existence of anyone called Big Fella and shut the door in his face, when Chas pushed me and my plan aside with a 'Fuck me!' and a bear hug.

Fight Three.

And this one was not going to be easily get-over-able.

While I washed Robbie's hands several times and then put him to bed, Chas yapped to Billy Mullen, who scared me with his bruised, cut, alien-like skull and constantly descending jeans (for the purpose of showing off infected machete scab, which he revealed on three separate occasions – to Chas, to me, and to Robbie, who TOUCHED IT!).

Chas turned into an alien too. After I put a resisting Robbie to bed, I listened at the door to the sitting room for a moment and noticed that Chas's accent had even changed. A posh Edinburgh boy who'd gone to private school and played tennis, Chas was using words like 'reccy' and laughing at Billy's stories of lucky buckets and peters. Who was this man?

I went and steamed in the kitchen for an hour while they drank five bottles of beer each and laughed so loudly I was sure they'd wake Robbie up. I stomped past the living room door at least twice and they didn't flinch. Then I spent ages trying to set up the ancient video recorder because *Build a*

New Life in the Country was on and I was going to miss it. They didn't even try to help me.

'Are you kidding me?' I yelled at Chas when the noxious weed that was Billy Mullen finally left.

'What?' said Chas, mystified.

'How can you bring him in here?'

'He's a fab wee fella,' said Chas.

'He's a fab wee fella!' I mimicked him, as if I was still in Primary Four.

'You're a snob and a pain in the arse,' said Chas, his face furious as he reached for his coat.

This was the first time Chas had called me a pain in the anything.

'You're not walking out,' I shouted as he fumbled to get his coat on, to do the 'time out' thing.

'I am, actually.'

'How can you call me a pain in the arse?'

'Easy. You are,' he said, unclenching my hand's grasp.

'Don't walk out on me. Let's sort this out,' I pleaded.

'If I have any more sorting out conversations, I'm going to explode. It's like I'm living with a fucking therapist.'

This was a surprise. I'd thought this was the thing that differentiated us from Zara's mum, and Marj from my old work, both of whom never talked to their partners about anything. Zara's mum had even weathered one argument by leaving notes on the fridge for three weeks and Marj only conversed with her revolting husband about what kind of meat he might like for dinner.

'In the last couple of weeks I've done nothing but look after Robbie and get it in the neck from you when I'm not in the middle of hour-long conversations about how the fuck we can make things better.'

'So you've done nothing but look after my son?'

'I didn't say that,' he snapped back.

'Well, if you don't like it, Chas . . .'

'All I did tonight was have a drink with an old friend who happens to come from a different socio-economic background. And you can't handle it.'

'He's an offender, and I'm a probation officer. Robbie's sleeping and you're swearing in there and drinking beer!'

'Oh my God!' said Chas. Then, instead of taking me in his arms and promising to change his character and personality forever because I was right and he was wrong, he added, 'You're a snob and a hypocrite.'

'A snob? *Me?*'

'And you're fucking naïve, Krissie. You take things at face value, believe shit just 'cause of how it looks. You're gullible, Krissie. You're a naïve, gullible snob.'

'*I'm* gullible! I know these guys, I *work* with these guys. They're dangerous. And you've just finished parole, Chas! Not to mention having him here is unprofessional!'

'He was by far the funniest guy I met in prison. If you can't tolerate the company of a boy from across the river in our house then you're in the wrong job *and* the wrong relationship.'

Before I could say anything in response, he was out the door.

And so was I, following him down the stairs and making a racket, not caring what the musicians downstairs heard, or what the old lady across the landing thought.

'Come back here, Charles!' Charles was a bad sign. I never called him Charles.

'Get back here now or –'

He stopped at the second landing and looked up at me.

'Or what, *Kristina?*'

'Or I'll . . . just get back here.'

But he just turned and walked away, and a few moments later I heard the door slam.

TWENTY-SEVEN

The next day I scrawled an angry, ridiculous letter of resignation. Robert and Penny were away facilitating a domestic violence workshop, so I was alone in the office with Danny.

'How does this sound?' I said, reading the letter to him.

Before Danny could respond, I put the letter down and got on my high horse.

·It had to be more than a coincidence, I told him, that my life had fallen apart as soon as I started work as a criminal justice social worker. There was the stress of working with admin staff who were mean witches from hell, refusing to help you no matter how difficult not helping might be in comparison. There was also the stress of having a boss who was never there, who left notes and reports and case files in pigeonholes in the early hours of the morning and then disappeared to fucking absentee management training of all things. And the stress of clients who were drunk or rude, and who refused to leave the interview room until you'd given them money or a cigarette. And the stress of abandoning my child to various places and carers all over the city. Plus the fucking stress of being the breadwinner . . . Of my boyfriend being away all day, all night, doing God knows what – maybe even fucking someone else. Of smoking again and having a terrible headache and only a day to complete a report on a man who bit another man's ear off and a never-ending pile of frigging whites . . .

'Stop!' shouted Danny.

What a relief, to be told to stop. My face had gone red with lack of breath and I was incapable of stopping alone.

'Breathe,' said Danny. 'Your life is not in ruins. You are tired and you had a fight with your boyfriend. Give me the report. I'll do it. And go home,' he added, before ripping up my attention-seeking letter of resignation.

That night Chas and I didn't sort things out, didn't have the chat that differentiated us from other couples. Instead we withheld affection and sex and I realised we were exactly the same as every other couple; that my gloating feeling of superiority was ill-founded.

Our chemicals had obviously done their stuff – two years was the limit, apparently – and we no longer tingled at the thought of each other or found each other's little habits cute.

I found the way Chas sometimes picked at his toes not cute at all. Ditto the way he worked all night in his studio and refused to show me any of his paintings. Double ditto the way he used my Mach Three razor and not one of the three I had bought especially for him. Not to mention the way he cooked nothing but pizza and that an overflowing washing basket was invisible to him. Or how he made me feel stupid because he was always so reasonable and invariably right.

They say the thing that attracts you to someone is the thing that will tear you apart. I'd fallen in love with Chas because he was down to earth and kind, because he didn't care what others thought of him, and because he treated people well, regardless of their looks or background. And indeed it appeared that this might be the problem, because I did not want him associating with Billy Mullen. It made me uneasy. I had a distinctly bad feeling about it.

We made sure Robbie had no idea of how estranged we were. I did the bath, Chas did the story, and we both lay on either side of him for a few minutes at bedtime before retreating and resuming our silent argument.

I ate my lonely Sainsbury's microwaved Thai curry in the kitchen, did the dishes, swept and mopped the floor, tidied the bathroom, put a load of washing on the pulley and another one in the machine, arranged the clothes for the morning, put videos in their cases, and did a list in my head of all of the above and a list of all the things Chas had done (i.e. nothing). Then he came in and declared: 'Let's have a party.'

'Sorry?'

'Let's have a party on Friday. Your folks are happy to baby-sit.'

'Your opening is next week, Chas.'

'I need to chill out. I want to have a drink and a chat and I want to flirt with you at a party and feel young again.'

'I don't feel like having a party.'

He knew I hated parties. I got stressed just thinking about organising them, which was one of the reasons I hadn't wanted to get married until an accidental wedding-dress purchase had fucked with my head.

'That's a shame. I've already invited some folk over.'

And off he went to fritter about in that fucking studio which could have been full of bare-breasted ladies for all I knew.

I didn't sleep at all as I tossed and turned and wondered what he was doing, and how we would ever get through this. When he came in and saw I was still awake, he said, 'You're stressed. You're not coping. We need to make some big changes.'

I lay there silently wondering how to bring up the list I'd made earlier of all the things I'd done in the house and all the things he'd not done, and how to say that a party was not a good idea and . . . I was the one with the problems. ME!

He sighed at the silence and left to sleep on the sofa.

Fuck.

This was not us. We were not this couple.

Fuck.

TWENTY-EIGHT

Leaving a maternity ward empty-handed is an unimaginable experience. Ask anyone whose baby has been placed in a tubed plastic container to grow some more, or been removed for detox and foster care. Ask anyone who's had a stillborn baby or a baby that died soon after birth. Ask anyone who's given up their baby for adoption. Not pleasant, walking with the limping gait of a torn new mother, alongside women with stomachs or little car seats filled with baby, smiles that are filled with baby, baby, baby.

Bridget Garden, just seventeen years old, walked out of the maternity ward empty-handed, her breasts hard and lumpy, wet patches on her T-shirt. She was still bleeding into the extra-strength super-size pads provided by the hospital – and continued to do so for as many days as the milk persevered. Her body cried a grief-soup of milk, blood and tears that would discolour her heart until she died.

When she got home to the house at Ballon she went to bed. She just lay there, body oozing.

Bridget's mother became increasingly worried about her daughter's mental health as the days passed.

'Let's go for a walk,' she would suggest, opening the curtains each morning. 'Or would you like to go to the movies? Bridge, please. Look at me. Talk to me. I'm sorry you're hurting, my little girl. I'm so sorry.'

For weeks, months maybe, Bridget lay in her bedroom with the lights off and the door shut, hoping for the healing that her mother insisted time would bring. But time did not heal. Instead the emptiness of a seven pound eight ounce child who had nuzzled into her ribcage grew – as if she were really there; it grew larger and heavier until it weighed on her so painfully that Bridget's mother realised she'd made a big mistake.

But it was too late. Something had been signed and someone had double-checked while Bridget had lain waiting for time to heal, and it was too late. The baby was someone else's, the life of motherhood, of watching and knowing and loving, was someone else's. A winning ticket thrown away.

Bridget put her name on a list and started her time. Eighteen years minimum, it would be. It was up to the little one she'd named Jenny. A sing-song simple name. Jenny.

As time wore on, there were many things that cushioned the sadness of losing her child. Bridget buried herself in her degree, and excelled. She chose a specialism that excited her, and loved her job. She chose to work and live near her family and friends, which meant she had the support of people who understood her loss.

And she had Hamish.

Bridget refused to see him for many months. But he persevered, ringing her daily, and knocking on the family door at least once a week.

'I'm sorry,' he said when she finally let him in. 'I'm so sorry. I love you.'

He was a kind and honest young man. They could never just be childhood sweethearts. In Hamish's arms, the burden of Bridget's grief seemed to halve. She loved him and she needed to be with him for the rest of her life.

It took years before they could contemplate having another baby, and they never discussed it. But one day Hamish didn't put a condom on and Bridget didn't complain. Afterwards, Bridget cried.

'I can't. I shouldn't. It's wrong to want this,' she said.

As usual, he told her what she needed to hear. They were so young when it happened. It was a terrible mistake, but they had to move on. Little Jenny was with a good family. They must try and be happy.

As Bridget's period arrived each month for the next year, her guilt and self-loathing turned to desperation and excitement. She wanted and needed to get pregnant. And eventually, she did.

Rachel. A blessing from God. A different girl. A fresh start.

But sometimes the pain returned and Bridget felt as if she was just going through the motions of life, getting into the routine of it, taking turns with the rubbish, ferrying Rachel to athletics, shopping in B & Q on the weekends, and all within the Ochil Hills that would be her cell walls for at least eighteen years.

TWENTY-NINE

Drink never makes things better for me. If things are bad, it makes them worse. I can only drink when a hundred per cent absolutely happy, and on the night of the party I wasn't even close to ten per cent happy.

Chas and I had not spoken since Fight Three. We'd played home tag. I'd come in, he'd go out. He'd sleep on the sofa, I'd sleep in the bed. He'd take Robbie to the park, I'd watch television. I'd take Robbie to the soft play area, he'd go to the studio. It was a terrible period of fear, loathing and very poor party planning, which resulted in a last minute dash to Marks & Spencer's and Oddbins and Mum and Dad's and about seventy phone calls to friends I'd lost touch with since my life had been sabotaged by two males and a prison.

The other problem on the night of the party was my nerves. I was really worried about our oddball mixture of friends milling about my house not getting on. I drank three vodka and tonics to ease the worry and by eight o'clock I was drunk.

Which made me more miserable and more nervous, especially when the oddball recipe of friends arrived:

There were the Posh mums with low-cut jeans, ironed hair and new kitchens just installed or just about to be; the Hippy mums who'd read very good books lately; the working mum's who wished they had time for kitchens and reading; the school friends who wanted to talk about Sarah's death, which I didn't; the ones who were surprised at how well I'd turned out, and those who smirked at how badly.

Then there were the friends of Chas's from medical school

who could never drink enough to disguise how boring they were; one very attractive female sculptor from the studio in Hillfoot; a ragtag assembly of Scottish socialists still wearing the same sort of clothes they wore in first year; a scattering of ex-Scottish socialists now living in very big houses; one gay cousin; an ex-shag from downstairs and his psychotic musician friend; the chick I cleaned with at the leisure centre during Uni holidays who liked me in my uniform and still liked me, I could tell; three heavy smokers from the New Gorbals netball team that I'd accidentally joined that morning; a colleague whose blindness made several mums (from category one, especially) ill at ease; two neighbours whom I'd never talked to before; social workers who had a lot to say about the demise or not of multiculturalism and that murder in the borders and hill-walking at night wearing nothing but a hat and that new hot hunnies bikini car wash in the deepest darkest East End and baking cakes with real butter and staplers and Robert Frost and was it okay if they took another teeny line of speed in the bathroom?

And Billy Mullen, who arrived just as I'd started dancing to music that was not cartoon- or nursery rhyme-related. After Chas welcomed him, Billy Mullen honed in on Marj (ex-colleague) almost immediately, even though she was married, admittedly unhappily.

Gradually, the vodka started doing its stuff, fuelling the mind with truths that had to be acted upon – now.

'We're not talking!' I said, walking up and putting my arm around my man after he'd talked for too long to the good-looking sculptor.

'That's a shame,' she said.

'It is a shame, isn't it, Chas?'

He didn't answer, though he did touch my hand.

'He's not talking to me because I talk too much,' I said.

Chas's hand gripped mine a little tighter than it had been.

'He's got a very big cock,' I said to the speechless sculptor girl who wasn't so good-looking up close. She had a straw-berry nose, needed microdermabrasion.

'What do you sculpt, then?'

'I'm working on a large ball made entirely of wire.'

I laughed so hard it nearly killed me. A large ball made entirely of wire! I couldn't believe it. When I finally stopped laughing, I felt distinctly left out, so much so that I wondered out loud . . .

'You've had it in your mouth!'

'Sorry?' asked the wire-ball girl.

'His cock!'

'That's enough, Krissie!' said Chas, dragging me away.

'You have!' I slurred. 'And the worst of it is, that he'd have seen your nose from up there, with all its huge fucking craters! Serves you right, you fucking wire-ball cunt!'

Chas slammed the door and we were on the close where the old bag woman called Mrs McTay from across the land-ing was perched for the evening's entertainment.

'It's my fucking party!' I started, not to be pacified by Chas, who was such a stranger to me now.

'Krissie, calm down. Stop and look at me. Eyes, into mine. I want to tell you why I organised this party.'

'Because you're bored with me.'

'Listen to me.'

'Leave me alone, let me back in.'

I pushed past him.

'Do you promise to be civil?'

'Not only do I promise to be civil, I promise to make a proper effort with your little friend Bobby.'

'Billy,' Chas said, taking the bottle of vodka from my hand and then moving away from the door.

I searched all over the flat for Billy Mullen and eventually found him in the shower with Marj. I turned the shower off to extricate them and they screamed and then laughed, and then Marj got out not worrying about the fact that you could see her hugely erect nipples through her wet white dress.

'I want to be your friend!' I said to him.

'Good,' he said to me, and that was it. We were friends. Friends who had nothing more to say to each other whatsoever.

I skittered around after that and Billy Mullen got people posing for the new Sony digital camera he had probably stolen earlier that day.

Peeping in on the mothers, I was in time for the following exchange:

ZACH'S MUM: Yes, well Zach did a full length with Euan, who's very good, doesn't take any nonsense, like the one you still use, Amelia.

PETER'S MUM: Peter's improved, you know. He can do fifty metres freestyle now and tumble turns.

ZACH'S MUM: Tumble turns? That's an odd thing to be teaching a three-year-old.

PETER'S MUM: He's four.

ZACH'S MUM: He's gorgeous, such a lovely boy.

PETER'S MUM: He's very well behaved in the pool.

ZACH'S MUM: No more of that pooing on the fountain then?

PETER'S MUM: That wasn't Peter!

I found myself impelled forwards, pressing my finger over the defensive mouth of Peter's mum and saying, 'Shh! Stop talking about fucking swimming lessons for fuck's sake. It's more boring than being dead. Haven't you got anything else to talk about? Fucking hell, it's like your minds are heavy sodden nappies and all you can talk is fucking pish.'

Thanks to me, the mothers now had something other than their children to talk about.

I grabbed another drink and found Robert, who was doing a line of speed in the bathroom with Billy Mullen and Marj. I waited my turn, snorted a line, and then moved even faster around the party to the mothers, who were leaving and not saying goodbye; the doctors, who were dribbling on about Tuscany; the socialists, who were not sharing so much as a conversation; and Chas, who was sitting on our bed with his knees almost touching the wire-ball girl's.

I saw red, literally, and then I saw Danny making his way along the corridor and I raced after him.

'Touch it!'

'What?'

'My face, go on. You know you want to.'

He was a bit pissed too, so he smiled and put his hands in the air. I took hold of them and placed them on my face and then I wondered what should happen next.

'DJWOOO GHWANNA NETT JOO NOO?'

I was asking him if he wanted to let go now and his hands were over my mouth and I may have wet his fingers a little, but he got the drift and let go, leaving us both dangling there, in the hall.

'I'm off,' he said, and I looked into the bedroom again and saw that Chas and his girl were huddled together, unaware of anything but each other. I grabbed Danny and I kissed him.

'You're a fucking idiot, Krissie.'

The funny thing was, this didn't come from Chas, or wire-ball-girl – they hadn't budged, and had no idea I'd just thrust my tongue in someone's mouth – but from Danny, who walked towards the door, opened it and left.

THIRTY

The honeymoon got worse and worse for Amanda. She'd spent two nights alone, and Jeremy was still in London hoping to see his sick mother. She had no car. And the families in boats grated on her to the point that she'd considered pulling one of the lock levers while no one was looking. What was she supposed to do? Read all those political histories? Watch a kids' DVD? Walk up the wet green hill in the pouring rain only to walk back down again? Think?

Amanda took the last option. She sat and thought for many hours, the last few of which were spent hovering over the payphone with her forehead lines at their deepest.

'Good morning, Family Finding,' came a chirpy voice.

She hung up and rang Jeremy instead. He sounded grim. He'd been down in London two whole days and his mother was still refusing to see him. And he was still refusing to give up.

'Do you want to come down here with me?' he'd asked last time she phoned. 'This is silly. We can have the honeymoon another time.'

'They might discharge her today, yeah?' said Amanda.

'That's what they said. I'll phone as soon as I hear anything,' he said.

Amanda returned to her staring position above the phone. It was looking at her, beckoning, saying, *You'll be leaving forever.*

To a new life.

Gone from Scotland.

Last chance.

Pick me up. Go on. Do it.

It wasn't that she didn't want to leave Scotland – she did. She loved Jeremy. He made her feel happy and they had fun together. But coming home made her realise that it is okay, good even, to understand who you are. She still didn't entirely understand who she was, not fully. Getting married and coming home and contemplating having children for the first time had awakened a desire to find out more about her parents. Was her wildness nature or nurture? Did she have siblings or half-siblings? Was there any history of mental illness in her family? Were her family all ginger (God forbid, she and Jeremy had admitted to each other).

All she knew, as told to her by her very kind and sensible mum and dad at the age of six, was that she was adopted and no less loved for it.

She picked up the phone and dialled again.

'Good morning, Family Finding.'

This time she didn't hang up.

'My name's Amanda Kelly,' she started, hardly able to believe she was actually making the call. Her voice trembled as she explained her situation. Her whole body trembled as she waited for the social worker to check things out and call her back.

She jumped when the phone rang.

'You should come in,' said the social worker. 'I've got a space tomorrow afternoon.'

Afterwards Amanda phoned Jeremy but couldn't reach him. She was going to tell him all about what she was doing. He'd known it was on her mind anyway, had even suggested they go through it together, but his home number rang out and his mobile went straight to voicemail. He was probably at the hospital, she thought. Shit, she could really do with hearing his voice.

So she didn't talk to anyone about what she was doing

before the appointment. She felt too guilty to tell her parents. They wouldn't discourage it, but it would upset them. When Amanda had brought it up ten years ago, over dinner, she could tell by the look on their faces that it was best not to.

That night, she lay awake wondering what the appointment might mean for her. Maybe nothing. Maybe everything.

In the morning, she drank three cups of strong coffee, filed her nails and got dressed. Jeremy had taken the car, so Amanda got the bus to Oban, which wriggled around the coastline for hours. Under any other circumstance it would have been spectacular, but Amanda didn't give a shit for views at the best of times, and especially not that morning. She arrived in Oban and walked to the car hire place on the outskirts of town, her adrenalin working its way up for each leg of the journey. And by the time she arrived at the Family Finding Office in Glasgow her heart was pounding so hard it hurt.

She stood at the front of the large ugly council building and took a deep breath. Did she really need to know? What would she find out? How would she feel afterwards? Taking another deep breath, Amanda put aside these questions – ones she'd asked over and over in her head for many years – and walked into the building.

It flipped her out afterwards how easy it would have been, for years, to do it. Her mother's name was on a database, had been since Amanda was twelve months old. Her birth mother had wanted to see her for the longest time.

The counselling was lengthy and forgettable. A matter-of-fact social worker told her about the ongoing support they could offer her. She explained that a reunion would be difficult and confusing, and suggested she should talk to someone close to her about it before deciding what to do.

'You shouldn't rush into anything,' said the social worker,

handing over leaflets and website addresses. 'Think, talk, prepare yourself for all possible outcomes.'

Amanda's head was all over the place, and all she wanted to do was get the piece of paper from the woman with the name of her mother, the details of her current address, and run out of the door and . . .

Finally, after a lot of nodding and pretending to be completely cool about it all, she was out of the door, the piece of paper in her hand, with no idea of what to do next. She sat in the car for several minutes just holding onto it, and the words that would tell her what she needed to know.

Then she looked.

Her birth mother – Bridget Garden then, Bridget McGivern now – had been seventeen when she was born. There were no details of the father. Bridget was five foot eight, the same as Amanda, and had red hair, shit. She'd been a medical student at the time of her birth. Her address had been 24 Wood Street, Ballon, when she'd given her up, and she was now living at 87 King Street, Stirling.

Amanda held the paper in her hand and looked at the fine black print that was the definition of her mother and herself all those years ago. Little black letters put together on a page, *meaning* her. She didn't cry. It would have been a relief to, but it didn't come.

What she did instead was to drive.

To Ballon.

THIRTY-ONE

That went well! I thought, hiding my face in my hands when I came to on the sofa the morning after the party. There were several people lying on the living room floor, red wine stains on the carpet, left-over cigarettes and joints in saucers all over the place, bottles and empty crisp packets and about twenty foil containers with half-eaten lamb bhoona and chicken tikka masala, and no Chas.

And no Robbie, who I was supposed to collect at twelve. Shite.

I rushed into my bedroom where, to my horror, Billy Mullen and Marj were lying naked. Then I rushed towards the bathroom where someone I didn't even recognise was taking a bath.

I grabbed some clothes and scraped them on, then got a taxi to Mum and Dad's house.

I hated myself. Drink had shown me to be an aggressive swearing blob of self-destructive obnoxiousness. I would never drink again. I was an idiot from hell with a hangover that throbbed and shrunk me to the size and mental capacity of a gnat.

As I poured myself into Mum and Dad's, I resolved to be more like them: fresh and smiley and soup-eating; or like Robbie, rosy-cheeked, uncomplicated and lovable.

Dad chauffeur-drove us back to the flat, which I hoped to God was empty apart from Chas.

And it was, empty, thank God, but there was no Chas.

Noticing the flashing answering machine, I hit the button, panicking.

'K, I'm going to stay at the studio till the opening. We need some space.'

The love of my life needed space. No wonder. Why would he be there? Why wouldn't he run a mile?

What *was* there, on the wooden floor in the hall, was an envelope filled with photographs printed on A4 paper. Photographs of me at the party . . .

Smoking a joint (when did I do that? I couldn't remember) . . .

Kissing Danny . . .

Snorting speed . . .

Underneath the photographs was a letter, from Billy Mullen, saying:

Hi Krissie,
I'm really glad we're going to be friends.
xx

THIRTY-TWO

The drive took forty-five minutes. Ballon was a posh little commuter town with beautiful large houses and more restaurants than shops. It was late afternoon, and the place was empty apart from ladies who coffeed. Amanda wanted to see the place her mother had been living when she gave her up for adoption, to see the house she might have grown up in. Wood Street was just behind the main drag, and number 24 was a semi-detached blonde sandstone house with a picture-postcard garden. The storm doors were locked. The owners, whoever they were now, were out.

Amanda's mother, Bridget, had lived here when she was seventeen.

Amanda looked at the house as a child would look at a wrapped present found hidden upstairs. Those curtains might have been her curtains, with their rope ties and aubergine pelmets. That window might have been her window, and she might have popped out from it and yelled to a friend on her way to school, 'Wait for me, wait for me!' That tree might have been her tree, to climb, hide in and smoke behind. A smell she'd never smelt might have wafted from that kitchen, of a meal she'd never had on a plate she'd never chipped. She scrutinised her parallel life – that present she had never shaken, let alone opened.

Eventually, the tears came. The car trembled with them. Alone in a silver Polo in a commuters' street on a Friday morning, she cried.

Amanda must have started the car at some point, and she wasn't sure how it turned itself off. Did she forget what to do next, and turn it off herself? She wasn't sure. All she knew was that she couldn't leave that place, so she didn't. All day she sat in the car, crying on and off, turning the car on and off (or not, she couldn't remember), and discovering new things about the house. It became comforting almost, watching an empty place and imagining.

So she was a little taken aback when a car slid into the driveway quite fast and stopped.

As did her breathing.

She watched intently as the door opened and a woman got out. A good-looking woman in her late sixties with several shopping bags and heels not made for walking.

Without thinking, Amanda got out of her car immediately, and raced over to the woman who was struggling to open the storm door and who was, without doubt, her tall, elegant grandmother.

'Excuse me!' she said to the woman, scaring her to death. She'd opened the storm door, and was now struggling with the inner one.

'My goodness! You scared me to death!'

'I'm not selling anything.'

'Good,' said the woman, ''cause I'm not buying anything.'

'Can I help you with the bags?'

'No.'

'I'm sorry, this is . . . My name's Amanda.'

'Uh-huh?'

I must have had another name, back then, thought Amanda.

'Yesterday I went to the Family Finding place in Glasgow, and I got this address.'

Amanda had practised the words she'd use on meeting her blood relatives. Statements like *I am your daughter* or *You are my mother* or *You gave me away* . . . and the like. She'd also imagined the possible reactions. A phone hanging up on her. A door being slammed in her face.

Her words had not been dramatic, but the reaction was one she rarely dared to dream of. The woman dropped her bags, put her hand over her mouth, and then grabbed Amanda by the shoulders and hugged her with all her might, saying, 'Oh my God! Oh my God!'

She was welcome. It was going to be okay.

Eventually, Amanda extricated herself, tears in her eyes, and said, 'You're Bridget's mother?'

'Yes, yes. Yes,' said the woman, holding into Amanda's arms, tears streaming down her face. 'I'm your grand-mother.'

THIRTY-THREE

Bridget had been eating a salami and humus sandwich which was rather dry and had thrown in the crusts in the bin because the days of feeling childish and guilty about not liking crusts had long gone. She was forty-five, and looked even younger. Reddish-blonde straightened hair and with perhaps a touch of Botox, or else a very lucky sun-deprived complexion. She wore suits all the time – skirt suits with well-matched shirts and jackets – and wedges. She was beautiful. Large blue eyes with a hint of sadness, a full well-glossed mouth and a slim physique. Her patients and her colleagues fancied her – men and women. In fact, the only person who didn't fancy her was her husband, Hamish, and that wasn't out of badness. Since the incident, as they called it, they'd only really had sex to make a second chance, Rachel – who was now eighteen and still living at home – and neither of them questioned it too much, or worried. Fancying each other wasn't a good thing, not after what it had done to them.

Bridget was about to take another sip of her orange juice when the phone rang.

'Oh my God, Bridge, she's here!' her mother screeched.

'What?' said Bridget, bemused.

'Sit down sit down,' came her mother's booming, over-excited voice.

'I *am* sitting down. You sit down. Are you okay?'

'Bridge, you're not going to believe this. Your first daughter just walked up to the front door and she's sitting at the kitchen ta –'

Bridget left the phone dangling, her orange juice half drunk, a bite of crustless salami and humus sandwich on her desk, and ran out of her office, down the corridor, out into the hospital car park, fumbled with her keys, started the engine, and drove as fast as she could around the infuriating one-way system in Stirling. She sped along past the university, through a traffic jam in the high street of Ballon, left past Somerfield, and then right into Wood Street.

Parking, she took a quick look at herself in the mirror. Her hair, blonder than God had intended, was okay. Her face was sandwich-free, and there was nothing she could do to impress this person anyway, so why was she bothering to look at herself?

She'd imagined this moment for so long.

Every child in every street after it happened could have been her Jenny.

Once she'd been on a bus in London and had spotted a woman bumping her pram down some steps. She'd raced to the front of the bus and asked the driver to stop NOW because she had seen a flicker of red hair in that buggy, and the child was tiny, could have been five months three weeks old, just like Jenny. When the driver stopped she ran towards the buggy, one of her shoes falling behind her in the process, and grabbed the woman by the arm and stopped her. Looking into the pram she saw . . .

. . . a boy, much bigger than she'd thought, a year maybe. And the woman walked off with her child-full life without pressing charges.

Then there was the honeymoon in Prague where a five-year-old girl was getting her portrait painted on the bridge and wouldn't stay still, and she could see in the child's eyes something of her own. A faint vulnerability, a twinkle of good fun. The girl was American.

At the Science Centre in Glasgow. Rachel was five. Her first would have been fifteen. Was that her? Skulking behind a large group of children from Notre Dame with very bad acne but a well-put-together uniform?

She'd never know. All she'd do was wait, and on the fifth of May, every year on the fifth of May, post a birthday card, with no stamp and no address, 'To my wee ginger nut'. Just pop it in the post, watch it disappear, and then walk away.

She spent night after night, especially on the fifth of May, wondering where her firstborn was, what she was doing, what she was eating, who was loving her. Twenty-eight years waiting for the results of a biopsy, waiting for Higher exam results, waiting for a pregnancy to become a life, for a drink of water . . .

And she was checking her face for food, the waiting over, somehow. How had she managed this wait? What would life be like without it?

For Amanda, too, inside that house, the half-hour seemed longer than the years she'd wondered. Wondered how her mother could have given her away. And why. What had stopped her from keeping her?

She looked at the clock in the glamorous kitchen of her glamorous new grandmother and watched it move – that first five minutes, that second set of three minutes, the last two, then one, and suddenly a lifetime of wondering was answered with the creak of a door, some fast footsteps along solid oak flooring and an embrace that was inappropriate for strangers, but not for them.

Thank you, God, they both said inside during that first long embrace, thank you God . . . for bringing her back to me.

THIRTY-FOUR

What would have happened if I'd thrown Billy's letter in the bin? What if I'd ripped it into teeny pieces and scrunched it up in a ball and tossed it out the window? Would my problem have disappeared? This thing that could destroy everything – my job, my relationship, everything? Would it have gone away?

It was worth a try, I thought, so I ripped it, scrunched it, and tossed it first at the wall and then in the bin.

Robbie, meanwhile, raced into his room, where he emptied all the trains and tracks from a box onto the floor and started playing with them. He seemed desperate for his own things after a night away. He was getting cuter every day, his hair blonder and curlier, his mouth a huge expanse of teeth because he was always smiling. He'd had reason to smile. His mum and dad, until a few days ago, had been the happiest couple in the world. They'd done everything together – every meal was a sit-down affair, every walk to the shops was hand in hand with intermittent '1-2-3 Weeeeeee's!'. Bedtime was family cuddle time, after family story time. And baths were funny, filled with Santa beards and Teletubby slides. His life was good.

Now, these photos, of me kissing Danny in the hallway, snorting speed in the bathroom, smoking a joint, could ruin it all. This could be the moment when – if I was writing a report for Robbie in years to come because he'd been joyriding or fighting at the football – I would say 'Ah!' (to myself). 'Ah! So that's why you're the way you are. Your mother had an affair when you were three. She was a drug addict. And your stepfather, who loved you with all his heart, left, never to be seen again.'

I spent hours in an anxious haze, cleaning frantically and trying to entertain Robbie, who asked endless questions about his daddy's whereabouts.

'He's painting,' I said. 'He's very busy.'

After putting Robbie to bed, I rang Chas about a hundred times and left about a hundred messages. Talk to me, forgive me, I'm a nut job, shouldn't have drunk, first session in two years, sorry, talk to me, ring me, ring me, answer, pick up, are you with her, are you fucking her, sorry, talk to me, shouldn't have said that, had another drink, shouldn't have, am a nut job, talk to me, forgive me, you're with her, aren't you . . .

No surprise, really, that Chas didn't come home that weekend.

So I was left – after a bath with no Santa beards and bedtime with no family cuddle – with my photos and the torn-up letter that I retrieved from the bin and taped back together. I thought logically. What did it mean, this letter? What impact could it really have?

Would I lose my job? Would it matter if I did, considering the nosedive my life had taken since I started? Shite, I'd been more sympathetic to some prisoner than to my boyfriend. Perhaps it wouldn't be the worse thing if I worked in Sainsbury's, except we couldn't pay the mortgage. We'd have to move back to Mum and Dad's, get tenants in the flat again.

Actually, it was probably good that Chas hadn't answered his phone. After all, he'd just finished parole. The last thing he needed was to get involved in any kind of criminal behaviour. I knew him well enough to know how he'd respond. He was the kind of guy who took things into his own hands. Liked to sort things himself. Didn't trust the police, or the courts. If I told him, he'd do something stupid, and get himself locked up again.

Then there was the kiss with Danny. Chas hadn't seen my pathetic attempt to get him jealous at the party. Add this to my abusive alcoholic behaviour, and he'd never come back to me.

But I couldn't tell the police either. See paragraph above re job.

Which left me with one option.

On the back of the pithy note Billy had left was a phone number. The first few times I rang it there was loud dance music and a muffled sound of people talking or partying. I hung up when I heard this, had a small sip of wine and tried again.

'Aye?'

It was Billy.

'What do you want?' I asked.

'Now that's not very nice, is it, hen? After all, you phoned me.'

'What do you want?' I asked again.

He hung up this time.

I was relieved that he had. Maybe he didn't want anything. Maybe I was being silly, assuming he did, and the photos were just photos. After all, this guy, I thought to myself over another wee glass, was a friend of Chas's. Chas liked him, thought he was nice, just a wee funny guy who'd unfortunately become hooked on heroin and did the odd theft to fund it. Not a nasty guy, Chas said, not one of the big wigs, just a user.

The comfort of this thought was interrupted by someone knocking on the door. I peeked through the peephole.

Billy.

I put the chain on and opened it slowly.

'All you have to do is take this in to your friend,' he said, holding something towards me.

'Who?'

'Jeremy.'

'Bagshaw?'

'That's right, Jeremy Bagshaw. If you don't, he's dead meat.'

'What is it?' I asked, looking at two packets of cigarettes in his hand.

'What do you think?' snarled Billy.

'I'm going to call the police.'

'I wouldn't if I were you. Jeremy's getting fed up of that health centre. And you wouldn't want anything to happen to The Chas, now would you, not when he's been such a good dad to little Robbie.'

And then he was gone. Before I had time to *not* take something in my daft outreached hand, he was gone, and I was left with two cigarette packets that were heavier than they should have been.

I sat on the window sill of our tenement flat and looked out over the cricket club. The cigarette packets were in front of me on the ledge, daring me to touch them, open them, smell them. I was shaking. I was chain smoking. I was drinking a second bottle of red wine.

THIRTY-FIVE

On Monday morning, when I dropped Robbie at the nursery, the staff gave me the smirks they'd set aside for me since my repertoire of sex toys had appeared in the structured play room. Robbie raced off to play with his pal Mark without even looking back, and I handed his lunch to Miss Watson.

Despite the possible repercussions for me, Chas and Jeremy, I'd decided during my sleepless night to head to the police station and tell them everything. I had Billy's cigarette packets in the car, and was absolutely sure it was the right thing to do. Never play along, never do what they say, I told myself over and over. It's daft, not worth it, the stuff of very stupid people.

But just as I was opening the door of the nursery to leave, Miss Watson said: 'We'll need your signature if you want Robbie's uncle to collect him this afternoon.'

'Sorry?'

'Billy Mullen. He rang to say he was going to collect Robbie.'

I raced to grab a highly puzzled and alarmed Robbie, who protested loudly.

'He won't be staying . . . and Billy Mullen is not Robbie's uncle. Don't let him in, whatever you do.'

I dropped Robbie off at Mum and Dad's.

'Can you look after him till I find another nursery?' I asked. 'It's not working out there.'

'Of course,' Mum said. 'What happened? Is Robbie all right?'

'He's fine. It's just not the right place. Can I pick him up after my work? Chas is flat out.'

I sat outside their house in my car. I looked around the street. There was an old man walking a dog, two youths skiving off school, a cat.

I dialled Billy's number carefully. I had to try. Maybe if he heard my voice he would find it in his heart to be a good person and not an evil one from hell.

'Please. Leave him alone. Leave us alone. Please.'

He paused before replying, and I felt a brief glimmer of hope, but then he said, 'Listen, it's just once, I've been promised that. Just the once. All you have to do is slip it to him. Put it in between some files or something. Lawyers get away with it all the time. Then, I promise you, this will all go away.'

'If I don't . . . If I go to the police . . .' I ventured.

'I can see you, Krissie. You shouldn't smoke.'

I looked around me. Shit, where was he?

'. . . Robbie looks so cute in red.'

I peered in Mum and Dad's window. Dad had Robbie in his arms and was dancing to something. Robbie had his favourite hand-knitted red jumper on.

Fuck, he was watching us somewhere. Behind that tree maybe? In that lane? He knew where I lived, where Mum and Dad lived, where I worked, where Robbie went to nursery, where Chas worked, everything, and could pounce at any moment and hurt my little boy, or my big boy. God help me, I couldn't ring the police or drive to a station because he was watching, ready to hurt, ready to kill.

'I know you'll make the right decision,' Billy said, then hung up.

I threw my cigarette out the window and rang work to say I'd be late, and drove straight to Chas's studio, which was empty except for a guy who was chipping away at a huge hunk of stone.

'He's gone shopping with Madeleine,' he said, in a not-terribly-friendly way. Clearly tales of my exploits preceded me.

So that was the wire-ball's name, Madeleine.

Shaking furiously, I drove at eighty miles an hour along the M8 to do what really stupid people do on the telly – people you yell DON'T! DON'T! at from your living room. Don't take them the million dollars, they'll kill her anyway, probably already have. Don't keep it a secret, tell people! Tell everyone!

If only there'd been people yelling at me from their living rooms. Maybe I'd have heard them, maybe I wouldn't have driven to Sandhill and parked where I usually parked, then gathered a few Jeremy-related papers and two files, given my name to the visits officer, left my mobile in a locker and put my handbag into the scanner.

But no one yelled at me and no one stopped me, and I did what daft people do, continuing on a lonesome path, thinking that visiting Jeremy was the only way to keep my son safe. Everything else was out the window by now. Losing my job and fighting with my boyfriend were irrelevant in the face of serious criminals making threats against my son.

Thank God the visits officer was not prone to small talk. I couldn't have managed a weather- or holiday-related conversation in a million years. I collected my bag at the end of the belt and walked into the glass cubicle to be transported to that other universe.

The door slid open, and I gave my name, walked to the waiting room, filled out a form – with Jeremy's name, prison number, my name, car registration – and then entered the Agents area. I'd been there many times in the last week, most of them for Jeremy, but also for James Marney, a drug user and a drink driver. I knew the score.

'Room 12,' they said, and I walked a little more confidently, my step getting less shaky, my grip less tight.

When I reached 12, I took my seat against the door of the room and waited, pretending to read over paperwork and shuffle through my things.

It took about fifteen minutes for Jeremy to appear. He looked a little better this time. The marks on his neck had gone down, the bruising on his face had mostly disappeared, and he seemed less vulnerable.

'What the hell have you gotten me involved in?' I demanded.

'What? What do you mean? Oh God, did Billy Mullen threaten you?' Jeremy said.

'Me, my partner, my son. Unless I pass gear on to you . . .' I paused and thought for a moment then took a deep breath.

'I'm not going to do that . . .'

(Come on now, I'm not that fucking daft!)

'Thank God,' said Jeremy. 'That's the last thing I'd want you to do. Shit, Krissie, I'm so sorry. I never wanted this to happen. That's what I meant about us both being in danger. I don't want the stuff. It's not for me. Billy's just looking for a way to get it in here. Knows you're visiting me, knows he can get right inside your life through your boyfriend, Baz, isn't it?'

'It's Chas. I'm sorry. I didn't know what to think. But we have to tell the officers. We'll do it together. You'll be placed on protection. It'll be okay.'

'We can't grass,' he said, fearful.

'He threatened to take my boy from his nursery. He's only three, Jeremy. I don't know what else to do, where else to go.'

'Can't Chas sort it out?'

'If he wasn't out shopping with someone called Madeleine.'

'I can take a beating, no problems at all,' he said. 'But I'm not going to let you get hurt, Krissie. You're the only one who's kept me going in here, and telling the officers or the police will make things worse for you, much worse. Believe me, I know who you're dealing with, this Billy guy. Listen to me. Get out of here and let me handle it. I couldn't bear it if anything happened to you because of me. I couldn't bear it if anyone else got hurt.'

He had tears in his eyes by the time he stopped talking, and I felt so sorry for him I wanted to hug him.

'Tell Billy Mullen I refused to take it. I'll sort things this end. I'll make sure you have nothing to fear, you hear me? You're safe.'

'Jeremy, you'll get *killed*.'

'Tell him. Tell him I said no, and if he wants to know why, he can deal with me direct.'

'What will I do with the stuff?'

'I don't know yet. I'll think about it. But don't tell anyone.'

I gathered my things to leave as he stood up, but before he got to the door I said, 'I think you're a good man, Jeremy.'

He didn't look at me, just stood at the edge of the door.

'I'm not a good man. I deserve to be punished.'

I sat in the car park of the prison, mind buzzing, white vans driving in and out, police vehicles driving in and out. What next? I wondered. Jeremy was right about grassing. In prison, it's worse than slashing or raping or being a beast. It's the unforgivable thing. And grassers never live long, not if they're dealing with the big yins. A year or so ago a prisoner told security a lawyer was bringing stuff in. They caught the lawyer. She's still doing time. The informer – a small-time shoplifter from Greenock – was found dead in the Clyde a week after his release. If Jeremy or I informed, we'd both end up underneath the same boat.

I dialled Billy's number again.

'He refused the drop,' I told Billy.

'What?'

'He refused to take it.'

'I don't understand,' said Billy, his tone bemused rather than threatening.

'I won't go to the police.'

'Good! That'd get you in even deeper shit. But I don't understand. What did he say exactly?'

'He said if you want to know why, you can deal with him direct.'

'Right. Fuck. I'll get back to you.'

Before I could say anything, he hung up.

I drove to work, hoping that Danny and Robert would be there, but Robert was out doing home visits and Danny was so monosyllabic and unforgiving ('Hi,' he said, without smiling) that I signed myself out on home visits, which I did, but not to clients.

First I visited my own home. It was dark, but clean after my frenzied sweep the night after the party. I put the heroin or cocaine or whatever it was in the plastic container I used for my secret stash of cigarettes. I shut the lid on the container tightly and did what I often did with horrible problems – hid it. After I'd placed the container back above the kitchen wall unit, I determined to forget all about it. Those cigarette packets did not exist.

Then I visited Chas's studio in Hillfoot again, an industrial space with scratchy walls, a skylight, a wee bathroom and a sofa in the corner. Chas had a room at the back of a gallery. It was filled with paintings leaning in towards the wall, hidden from view – canvas backs, bolts, wood and cloth the only visible elements.

I walked up the towards Chas's room and there he was, putting a flower in Madeleine's hair, then gazing at it. A tiny rose it was, attached to some kind of hair clip or wire. He was not working like a dog, which is what he was supposed to be doing. Not working and not crying about our argument or mourning the loss of me and our family, but putting a fucking flower in wire-ball Madeleine's hair and gazing at her.

I couldn't believe it. Chas had left me. He'd left Robbie. All this shite about us falling in love over and over and learning stuff about each other and not giving up on each other was total unadulterated bullshit.

I found myself walking over and staring at them in silence. They stared back, as if I should be the one to say something first.

'Hello,' said Chas, after a while.

'I've been having a lot of trouble,' I whimpered.

'It follows you around, Krissie.' His tone was not encouraging.

'Is it over, Chas? Are you sleeping with her?' I asked.

'How can you come in here and ask me that? God, this is typical of you, taking one tiny bit of information and flying with it as if it's the truth. When are you ever going to stop jumping to conclusions? Not everything is as it looks on the fucking surface.'

'What? Why are you being such a bastard? Who are you? I need you and you're scaring me.'

'I'm not being a bastard. I just need some space. You were out of control at the party, K, calling my friends cunts. You need to get your head together. And I need to get the opening over and done with. Just try and get your head together in time for the opening, okay? We can sort it all out then.'

He glanced at the sculptor, who smiled at him!

I wanted to punch things – him, her. They were a team, against me. My Chas, my life, who'd loved me always, was in a team with some other chick, right in front of me.

I tried to recall some anger management skills, time out, breathing, closing eyes. I tried, but instead I found myself getting the A4 photos out of my bag and flicking through

149

them and not showing Chas the really worrying drug-related ones, or the note, but the photo of me kissing Danny.

'Well, your friend took this photo to hurt us. So, as it turns out, I was right,' I said looking at the sculptor girl. 'Your friends *are* cunts.'

THIRTY-SIX

My relationship was obviously over. I howled on the way back to the office, and then tried hard to distract myself with work. I had a lot of it to do – an interview for a court report, calls to doctors and community service officers, appointment letters to clients, and case notes. So I got on with it as best I could, hoping that the distraction would take away the reality of my situation.

At five o'clock I switched off my computer and a sick feeling immediately overwhelmed me.

Chas had left me.

I still had drugs in my kitchen.

I needed to calm down, think things through a bit, talk to someone.

I needed a manicure.

Before going to collect Robbie, I found myself telling Amanda about Chas. She filed as she talked me down – a drunken snog at a party, stress, drink. It wasn't as bad as it seemed, she said, nothing to worry about. 'You just need a day to cool off. Just give him a day. Neither of you are going to lose what you have for a wee flirtation or whatever. It's trivial. You'll get through it. After all, it's not as if he's in Sandhill for murder.'

And it came back to me, a bird flying into a window, bang. Worker–client. And Amanda wasn't the worker (even though she was now gluing tips for money), she was the client, and at the end of the day Amanda would always be completely uninterested in anything I had to say about my own problems.

What also came back to me as Amanda turned the conversation back to her own hellish life was perspective – which wasn't a bad thing, to google 'famine' when you feel sorry for yourself – and I immediately snapped into a slightly less unprofessional role to focus on my client.

'Is there any news about the trial?' I asked.

'Not really. I'm just praying his mother will come to her senses. But I think Jeremy wants to be in prison,' said Amanda. 'He wants to punish himself. And he wants to protect me.'

'From what?'

Amanda hesitated, torn. But then her expression changed and I knew she was about to spill something important.

'I have to tell someone. God, I have to talk about it. It's driving me crazy. No one knows. No one but him,' she said, her eyes wet.

'What?'

'He doesn't want people to find out. He thinks it would hurt me too much. He thinks they'll assume I killed her, that it gives me a pick of motives: abandoned child, scorned lover, deranged deviant . . . God, maybe I am all of those things.'

'What are you talking about? Find out what?' I asked.

'I did something really strange. I can't explain it. When I think about it, I want to throw up. What sort of person am I?'

'Tell me what you did.'

'When I visited Jeremy after he was arrested, I told him,' said Amanda. 'I'd been alone in Crinan while he was down south, I was alone in that shithole of a place and so much had happened. He knew I'd found my natural mother on that second day, but so much else had happened that he'd had no idea about until I spoke to him in the police cell.'

'What else happened?' I said, intrigued.

'I can't say it out loud.' Amanda looked nauseous.

'Whisper it, then,' I prompted gently.

'It's too awful.'

'Just whisper in my ear.'

She looked around nervously, leaned in and whispered, 'I told Jeremy there was more to it, more to it than just meeting her, but he wouldn't let me explain to the police because he didn't want people to know.'

'What?'

She moved back, looked me in the eye, took a breath for courage, and said, 'He didn't want people to know that I'd . . . slept with her.'

'Slept with who?'

'With Bridget.'

'Bridget McGivern?'

'. . .Yes.'

THIRTY-SEVEN

Amanda had slept with her mother. Bloody hell.

I went back to the office and sat at my computer for a while, and was shocked to discover reams of research about adoption reunions, some of it arguing that up to fifty per cent can result in obsessive emotions and often in sexual attraction. It even had a name – genetic sexual attraction – and was a time bomb, apparently, with IVF and suchlike. There was a case in one country where a brother and sister, adopted to different families at birth, found each other and fell in love. They were forced to be sterilised.

After googling like crazy I began to understand it, an automatic and assumed physical closeness, intense, unyielding, but without the boundaries that come from dug-out roles that take slow years in the digging.

It wasn't as crude as an incestuous fuck. It wasn't abuse. It was clutching, melding, no time for thinking, no way to stop.

Still, bloody hell.

It was late. I had to collect Robbie.

Robbie had had a great day with Mum and Dad. They'd visited the park and the soft play area. He'd eaten well, and fallen asleep in Dad's arms at six o'clock.

'Can we have him overnight?' Mum asked. 'Seems mad to move him.'

I kissed Robbie's forehead and snuggled into his warm chest. My little bloss.

'Can you do me a favour, though?' I asked. 'Just lock the

doors and keep an eye out. There's lots of creepy people about.'

'This job's making you paranoid,' Mum said.

If only she knew.

'I love you guys,' I said, hugging Mum and Dad goodbye, wanting to tell them everything, but not wanting to worry them more. 'This job is a nightmare, but I think it'll get easier. Thanks so much for helping me out.'

I looked around me when I walked out the door. The street was empty. Robbie would be safe, wouldn't he? Anyway, where would be safer?

When I got home to my empty flat, I drank a whole bottle of wine in twenty minutes. With no food in my tummy, my brain turned to mush immediately and I found myself standing in the middle of the kitchen, thinking:

You have two choices, Miss Krissie Donald. You can STOP. Just stop for a moment and THINK. If you do this, you will see that Amanda's affair with her biological mother is of no consequence to you. You will see that Jeremy's unforgiving parents are of no consequence. You will see that his guilt or otherwise is of none either.

What IS of consequence to you, Miss Krissie Donald, is that there are threatening photos, a letter of bribery and two packets of drugs in your kitchen. Also of consequence is that the love of your life is not in your kitchen. He is with someone else, giggling. Easy. Two things to sort. Sort them out. Deal. Deal with THEM. One at a time. Write a list. One. Two. Then deal.

Was someone talking sense? If so, I'd stopped listening after the fifth glass of wine and started listening to a far more intriguing voice that whispered in my ear from my lonesome window sill, a voice that spoke to me of Jodie Foster and Hannibal Lecter, telling me to go and get the large blackboard from Robbie's room and place it in the middle of the kitchen floor with several half-used pieces of thick colourful chalk.

You're going mad, Miss K, the voice of reason persisted, but I quelled it with a red skull of liquid and, with the serious mouth of Ms Foster, wrote on the incident board of my new incident room:

Who killed Bridget McGivern?

I'd paid over £30 for unnecessary nail endeavours that afternoon while Amanda told me the most shocking story I had ever heard. Or was it? Was it more shocking than the one Jeremy had told me? Or Robert's one about the man with dementia and his well-hung three-legged dog? Well, at this point, two weeks into the job, it was my most shocking, I thought to myself, or at least an equal first. As such, it required discussion and thought and note-taking and some re-reading of theory like Oedipus and Schmedipus and Electra and abandonment and attachment and all that shite.

Who killed Bridget McGivern? I had written at the top of my incident board.

(Of course there is something to worry about. Take the drugs to the police, you fucking idiot . . .)

Jeremy? I wrote in column one.

(Ring 999 . . .)

Amanda's parents, Mr and Mrs Kelly? I wrote in column two.

(Beg Chas to take you back . . .)

Bridget's husband, Hamish?

(Grovel, get down on your knees . . .)

Amanda?

(Fuck's sake, don't open another bottle! . . .)

Bridget's other daughter, Rachel?

I AM CLARICE STARLING. I HAVE NO PROBLEMS IN MY LIFE OTHER THAN THE SOLVING OF MURDER MYSTERIES, THE FREEING OF INNOCENT MEN, THE

SAVING OF DUNGEONED HOSTAGES WITH STRAG-
GLY HAIR AND NO FOOD.

Shite, I thought to myself as I looked in the mirror later. Jodie didn't have grey teeth and a red stain on the right-hand side of her mouth, and she never cried in the mirror while snot ran down her face! Shite. Shite.

Bed.

THIRTY-EIGHT

Definitions need a set of conditions, or assumptions, to make sense – that touching someone who is spoken for is wrong; that blood relatives learn boundaries and rules over time. But for Amanda and Bridget there were no such conditions, no such assumptions.

Affair: illicit, secretive, sexual liaison.
Incest: sexual relationship between blood relatives.
Affair: secretive sexual liaison.
Mother: female parent.
Incest: relationship between blood relatives
Affair: liaison.
Incest: relationship.
incest illicit
affair
blood relationship
between secretive blood sexual relatives

The McGiverns had drinks to celebrate the arrival of their Amanda, the ginger-nut girl they had lost. The whole family arrived on that first evening to embrace her – uncle, father, sister. Cars arrived at the house and feet rushed along the oak floor taking turns to hold her, as they would have held her at the hospital if she'd arrived and stayed the normal way. They each looked her over, checked the eyes, the hands, the hair and the nose. There was hysteria, over-laughing, jaw-tingling crying. There was the wetting of the baby's head.

Nothing made sense, really. It was make-believe. At the start and at the end, Amanda felt like she was reading lines in a romantic comedy or a family drama or a thriller or a tragedy that was so mixed-genre and strange that it would never get made, but she took her script in hand and her role began – the affair that was not really an affair, the incest that was not really incest – she took her script and the make-believe began . . .

Day One

EXTERIOR, DETACHED SANDSTONE HOUSE, BALLON, STIRLINGSHIRE

It's sunny and spring. Daffodils stand yellow along the street. Well-to-do cars park in well-to-do drives.

INTERIOR, DETACHED SANDSTONE HOUSE, BALLON, STIRLINGSHIRE

Sunny and spring. Daffodils sit in deliberately bent glass vases on French-polished sideboards. A family laughs and cries as if at a wake. Amanda swirls around the room feeling the confusion that comes with fame – answering questions, being looked at, being checked out, being loved and wonderful and tingling. She swirls around and her face says this is the best day of her life, the happiest, the most exciting, the best by far.

She meets her uncle, a drunk in a kilt.

AMANDA
Hello, Uncle.
UNCLE
Hello, Amanda.

She meets her sister, a goth with an attitude.

AMANDA

Hello, sister.
RACHEL
Hello.

She meets her father, a teacher with a suit.

FATHER
Hi.
AMANDA
Hello. ·

And she meets her mother. A woman in a grey trouser suit with a white tailored shirt, black wedges and a set of black pearls, neat but not neat, pretty but more than pretty, smiling but not really, laughing but not really, a set of model features, model legs, model arms, model tits, model everything, and this was her mother? It didn't make sense. Her mother was a woman of seventy who lived in a concrete box and worked like a dog in a shit job and went to church and wore cardigans and made soup, and yet this was also her mother? This woman who could be her sister, who could be her friend, who liked the same things she liked, black olives and Thai crisps, and looked sexy, and when she laughed all of her teeth showing, and the lines around her eyes bunched together in celebration.

BRIDGET
Hello, Jenny.
AMANDA
Jenny?
BRIDGET
Can I call you Jenny?
AMANDA
No.
BRIDGET

What can I call you?
AMANDA
My name.
Bridget hesitates.
BRIDGET
Hello, Jenny.
FADE TO BLACK

That was how it began, Amanda's fucked-up movie. And it
ended on the fifth day.

Day Two

There was some explaining to do. The stuff you do after the
first meal out, when you talk over exes and find out if the
other is a heartless bastard, a needy cling-on, a proper
freakazoid.

Amanda and Bridget were at a restaurant in Bridge of
Allan and it was formal. Small tables with ironed cloths and
not enough noise. Couples sat miles apart, thanking the lord
that they were as they had nothing to say to each other
anyway, small bloody meat was piled cumbersomely onto
plates with sprigs and spuds in layers, and wine that cost £18
a bottle chilled in silver iced buckets. They had two bottles
and stopped worrying about the lack of noise after a while
because they had some explaining to do.

Well, it was Bridget who had to explain and she knew that
it was an impossible task, actually, explaining why she'd left
her, then married the man anyway and made a replacement.
There was no way of explaining that. Although she tried –
'I didn't know what I was doing . . .' 'I was young . . .' 'My
mother pressurised me, she knows she made a mistake
too . . .' But she couldn't justify having given Amanda's life
to two sets of people – first to the Kellys, that 'nice couple
in Glasgow that liked cats'. Bridget started . . .

'Puddles died,' Amanda said. 'She was run over by my school bus when I was seven. I felt the bump.'

(She wasn't going to make this easy.)

'And they liked holidaying in Spain?' Bridget continued . . .

'I got food poisoning. We never went back.'

'. . . Had a big extended family?' Bridget was wavering, but didn't know how to stop.

Amanda was silent. She wanted to be brat-like, angry, to say 'I hate them all', except she didn't; she really liked her large extended family, a lot.

'What's Rachel like?' Amanda asked. Rachel was the second person to have received the gift of Amanda's life, and Bridget sensed that this would be a difficult subject, and should perhaps be dealt with before rather than after two bottles of wine.

'I want to go home,' Bridget said, and the dynamic changed a bit. She wanted to cry, obviously, wanted to bang her hands on the sheets of her bed and weep, and Amanda realised that she also had some things to explain.

'I'm sorry. I had a very happy life and I don't hate you. I don't blame you and I don't want to argue about who did what when and all that bollocks. I just want us to be mates, if possible, and if that means we don't talk about stuff for a while, then so be it.'

They stayed for a third bottle and didn't talk about any of that stuff for a while.

They sat at the table and shared the same wine, ate the same food.

'I had nothing but ice cream when I was pregnant with you.'

'What kind?' Amanda asked.

'Chocolate Chocolate Chip.'

'Hagen Daaz?'

'Hagen Daaz . . . oops, sorry.' Amanda had accidentally

kicked Bridget under the table. 'You'd only stop moving about if I finished the whole tub.'

Amanda took some dessert from the laden spoon that Bridget had offered. 'It's so rich,' said Amanda as her lips moved the cake from the spoon to her mouth.

They ended up on the sofa of Bridget's living room. It was an even larger house than her grandmother's. Huge and posh and old, and the night lights around the gorgeous Stirling Castle filtered onto the garden and into the living room.

'I should never have left you, with your red hair all spiky . . .'

'I prayed for you, when I prayed . . . let my mum be safe and happy.'

'I still do.'

'Do you?'

'You're so beautiful.'

They were holding hands, stroking arms and cheeks, crying openly with no thought of tissues, when Hamish and Rachel walked in.

Rachel was eighteen. She was muscular and lean, obviously very fit, had taken to goth black clothing and make-up, which did added to her general air of discontent. She stood at the door with her arms crossed.

'Hi, Amanda,' Rachel said awkwardly as she beheld the women de-nestling and standing up guiltily from the sofa.

'How was the band?' her mum asked.

'All right. I'm going to bed,' she said.

'Goodnight, Rachel,' said Amanda.

After Rachel left, Hamish hovered at the door, wondering if he could leave too.

'Amanda's moving to London,' Bridget said by way of bringing Hamish into the conversation.

It couldn't have been more different, the reunion of father and daughter. Hamish felt nervous and uncomfortable, which made him business-like and back-patty. He didn't have an immediate connection with Amanda. She hadn't grown in his stomach, been pulled from his bosom, taken from his hospital room. She was a story he heard about later, one he had no say in but paid for as he watched the woman he loved grieve her loss. Jenny, Amanda, whoever she was, was a stranger to him. She made him feel uneasy. He should love her, the way Bridget obviously loved her. He should want to hug her, talk to her, feel sorry for her, get to know her. Instead, all he felt was worry: that Bridget would sink into depression again, that this stranger would make their happy family explode from within, that his beautiful Rachel would feel pushed aside.

Hamish asked whereabouts in London because he had stayed in Holland Park in 1988, or was it 1989. Anyway, it was very expensive.

It had been comforting, talking on the sofa with Bridget. But standing around in the formal living room was dreadful. Amanda felt ill to the stomach. She felt like a burglar, coming into these people's lives all of a sudden, going through their drawers.

'It's late,' Bridget said. 'We should both get some sleep after all the excitement.' She left Amanda to sleep, as planned, on the sofa.

'Goodnight,' Bridget said, hugging Amanda warmly and crying. 'Goodnight, my wee ginger nut.'

Amanda woke on the sofa at 6 a.m. and wrote a note before leaving in an awful hurry. She did not want to be seen on that sofa, did not want to talk to anyone.

'I'm at the Lock House by Crinan,' she wrote. 'My mobile's 555 978548. Thanks.' She was about to sign her name, but didn't. She didn't feel like Amanda any more, but she didn't feel like Jenny either.

'Mum?' The first thing Amanda did once she got back to Crinan was ring Glasgow. Her voice wasn't hiding anything.

'What is it, my darling?' Mrs Kelly asked. 'Are you okay? How's the honeymoon?'

Amanda had intended to tell her lovely mum, but she couldn't. She felt terrible, lying, but she knew she'd feel even worse telling the truth.

'It's fine,' she said. 'I love you, Mum, do you know that? I love you and I love Dad and you have given me a wonderful life.'

'Honey, what is it?'

'Nothing, Mum, PMT,' she lied. 'I just love you, that's all.'

'We love you too, honey. Have you got Evening Primrose?'

'I have. I've got it.'

'How's Jeremy?'

'Oh, he's down south for a bit. His mum's ill. He'll be back today probably. I'll tell him hi when I see him.'

'Is his mum all right? Perhaps that's why she felt she couldn't come up for the celebrations? Oh Mand, I wish you'd called sooner – are you all right by yourself?'

'Yes, she's fine, yes, no, I am too, I'm just tired and hormonal and he'll be back soon. He's a good man, Mum. I love him.'

'Take the Evening Primrose . . .'

'I will. Bye.'

'Bye, darling. Ring me again and drink lots of water. Your dad's just out in the garden and tell Jeremy to tell his mum we said to get better . . .'

'Will do. Bye, Mum!'

'Jeremy?'

'How did it go?'

'It was amazing, hard . . .'

Amanda had phoned Jeremy after the first meeting in Ballon. They'd talked for hours and he was everything she needed: understanding, kind, patient. He asked all the right things and offered all the right things and she felt safe and loved when she hung up.

'How's your mum?' Amanda asked.

'She's getting out soon. She knows I'm here, so it's been worth it, but she hasn't wanted to see anyone . . . I'll come up tonight.'

'No, listen, stay till she gets out. Have you spoken to her?'

'No, but maybe I'll get a chance when she's being discharged.'

'You should wait then.'

'Are you all right?' Jeremy asked. 'I'll come, I'll drive up now.'

'No, try and see your mum first. Anyway, it's kind of something I need to do by myself. Is that okay?'

'Of course it is, my love. Ring me any time, if you need to talk. And tell me if you want me there – I can be there in five hours. Promise?'

'I promise.'

'You'd think one of us could have a normal mother–child relationship!'

'Does anyone?' Amanda asked.

'I don't know.'

Day Three

Amanda knew Bridget would come. She waited by the window and watched the families watch the water rise and fall and she knew she would come, and she did.

There wasn't a particular moment when it moved from something suitable to something not. It wasn't one of them in particular who stroked an arm in an improper way, who lingered for too long after a cheek kiss. It was both of them, swimming in each other for those days, unable to remove their gaze from the other's eyes, attaching. It was if they had

166

been transported back to that moment twenty-eight years earlier when they lived on the same food and water, when they were suddenly naked and bloody together, then torn apart. They would not be torn this time.

Amanda started to understand the appeal of the country in the hours she spent with Bridget. Two whole days and two whole nights in the green, with no noise and no cars and no neighbours. Two whole days and two whole nights alone, together, to talk about the stuff they'd avoided earlier.

Bridget told Amanda about the weeks she spent in bed after giving birth, about how much she regretted her decision, and how hard she tried to reverse it. She told her about marrying Hamish at the local register office some years later, and how the love they had for each other was always clouded by the event that marked the beginning of their life together. She spoke about the guilt she felt at wanting another child and how this guilt might have affected the way she mothered her second born. When Rachel came out, Bridget said, her mouth seemed gnarled, and no amount of pillows in the right positions made mother and daughter work together. When a bottle was finally offered, Rachel gulped with desperation. Scary, almost, how she drank, and how peace only seemed to come from the plastic, and not from anything Bridget could do.

'Sometimes I think I was trying so hard not to see you when I looked at her, that I ended up failing the both of you,' said Bridget.

It continued this way. Through potty training and homework and Higher exams, Bridget felt useless in the teaching and in the comforting. It was her dad who could cuddle Rachel and find her other shoe. Her dad who could sit beside her and not be aware that their arms were touching.

All Bridget could do was tell her she loved her.

'You too, Mum,' Rachel would say.

Day Four

INTERIOR, LIVING ROOM, LOCK HOUSE, BY CRINAN, NIGHT

Bridget and Amanda are huddled on a leather sofa. A photo album with family shots of Bridget graduating and getting married is open on the table beside a half-empty bottle of whisky. Amanda holds Bridget's hand gently and files her nails, then puts the file in her lovely brown manicure set. She stops and looks at Bridget. Hair is stroked, eyes are looked into, and before they know it they find what was denied them all those years ago. The softness and fullness of it. Amanda unbuttons with a trembling finger, watches the response and invitation it gives her, and puts her mouth to it.

Day Five

INTERIOR BEDROOM, LOCK HOUSE, BY CRINAN, MORNING

Amanda lies awake and watches the woman beside her. Her breasts fall to the side slightly and her chest moves up and down with her soft breathing. She sleeps prettily, no open mouth or snoring, and she is naked.

Amanda creeps out of bed.

EXTERIOR, OBAN, MORNING

Amanda leaves the car at the hire depot. She looks down the road, in the direction of the Oban train station.

FADE TO RED

THIRTY-NINE

When Amanda saw Bridget next she was in a wooden box in the Dunblane cathedral.

She hadn't heard from any of her biological family since Jeremy's arrest. After all, if not for her arrival on the scene, Bridget might still be alive. She certainly wasn't invited to the service, and she had tried to keep away, but couldn't.

Creeping into the back of the cathedral, Amanda sat in an aisle seat. Upfront, she noticed the people she'd met in Ballon that first night – the drunk uncle and the sister and the father. She hoped they wouldn't turn around and see her. If they did, what would they do? What would she do?

Amanda looked at the coffin and thought: *I ruined that woman's life . . . twice. I brought her nothing but tragedy.*

And now she was in a box. Gone, again.

Lost, found, lost.

'A generous, loving woman, who gave everything to her family,' Hamish was saying at the pulpit, 'to her daughter Rachel and to me. A woman who gave up her teenage dream to work with Doctors Abroad to live a happy and settled life with the people she loved and cared about . . .'

She loved me too, Amanda thought to herself. *Didn't she?*

As the eulogy drew to an end, Amanda snuck out of the church. She was an impostor. She had always been an impostor. She longed to walk behind the pall bearers as they carried the coffin out, to drive in the main car, to stand at the front at the cemetery and throw dirt on the coffin. But she couldn't. Her rightful place in this woman's life, as always, was nowhere. Amanda walked down the steps of the cathedral, beside the empty hearse, and to her car.

She'd long been an atheist, but as she drove home she prayed out loud. She prayed that someone was listening. She prayed that Bridget was at peace. She prayed for forgiveness. She prayed that justice would be done, that her husband would be released, and that the police would find the monster who'd killed her beloved Bridget.

FORTY

Who killed Bridget McGivern?

FUCK! I had woken late, trudged my way into the kitchen and stubbed my toe on the blackboard I'd placed right in the middle of the room when I was pissed as a fart the night before. What a drunken idiot. Who killed Bridget McGivern? Incident room! Jesus Christ, I needed therapy. I needed detox and therapy. I also needed a drink of water because my mouth had been invaded by rabbit fluff that'd been mixed with rabbit shit and rabbit sawdust. I put the blackboard back in Robbie's room and brushed my teeth for seven minutes.

I'd never really experienced a proper break-up. I'd watched two friends go through it, though. One, Laura, was surprised by it on an unusually hot afternoon. She'd come home from work with an organic chicken to find him gone. Three years living in the same flat, never a hint of unhappiness, and all she had was a huge and extortionately priced chicken, which she still cooked, and this surprised me as much as his leaving surprised her. That she just got on with it, even roasted some potatoes Delia-style, which isn't easy, didn't run fast on roads looking for him, stand on bridges in snow begging, stay under her dark duvet till she was crusty. She just got on with it, let him go, like that.

The other friend wasn't surprised by it, because she orchestrated it. Bored with twice-weekly encounters and arguments over Sky+ management, Jane found it simpler to fuck the brains out of the guy at the corner shop than just politely ask her husband to leave.

I'd never experienced it because I'd never been in love, and I surprised myself, actually, because I never thought I'd be more sensible than organic Laura or Sky+ Jane, but I was. I was sensible, despite the previous night's madness, and I decided I would think this thing through and save it, which, I knew above all else, required the support and advice of my mother.

'Where's Chas?' Mum asked when I arrived at the door the next morning.

'Can I say hi to the Robster first?' I asked, kissing her.

Robbie and Dad were in the back garden. Robbie was digging a hole with his wee garden fork. 'I'm building a tree,' he said. 'Then Granddad's going to make a new tree house.'

'There's something wrong, isn't there?' Mum guessed when I came back inside. 'Sit down, have something to eat before you go to work. Where's Chas? Robbie says he paints all day and all night'

'We've split up!' I said, then cried and blew my nose melodramatically for quite some time.

'What? How? Tell me, darlin'.'

'I kissed someone at our party!'

Mum and Dad were long-suffering. I'd long been a difficult daughter. I'd always got into trouble as a kid, teenager, and now as an adult. They'd always been there for me, with words of comfort and advice, always at the end of the phone, on their way over . . .

Until now.

'Right Kristina, that's it.'

'Excuse me?' I said.

'You moved out less than a month ago and you've already stuffed it up?'

I bawled with resolve at this. Little did she know, I'd not just fucked up my relationship, I'd also:

- Become addicted to the manicures of the wife of a client, who was therefore by default a social work client herself – i.e. not to be confused with a friend or service provider.
- Become unprofessionally close to a (possible) murderer and (definite) client.
- Hugged said client/murderer in prison.
- Started drinking again. Too much.
- Started smoking.
- Not just tobacco, but joints, at parties.
- Snorted speed.
- Harboured Class A drugs.
- Sexually assaulted a colleague at a party.
- Endangered the life of my family as a result of all the above.

'How can you say that?' I yelled at her. 'How can you be so heartless?'

But she didn't back down, or sit down, or change her body language and tone to her normal motherly forgiving one. Instead, she stood over me with pointed finger and said: 'Chas has done everything for you, and you're a silly brash girl. Personally I don't think you *deserve* him.'

'But you said I did deserve him!'

'I've changed my mind since you've moved out! And I'm telling you, if you don't get off that self-obsessed arse of yours now and go beg his forgiveness, then I'll punch you in the face.'

'You will not,' I said, daring her tight face, which was mightily close to mine.

But she did. Without a moment's hesitation, she put her little mumsy hand into a fist and punched me on the nose, and while she gasped as if she had not intended to make contact, it bloody hurt, but more than that, it scared the shit out of me. Mum had never so much as smacked me on the back of the hand.

'We'll look after Robbie. You go beg that poor boy to come back, and tell him I said I don't blame him if he does-n't.'

She opened the door and waited till I was gone, slamming it in my face and leaving me and my tissue on the step.

What was I supposed to do? Go back to the studio again? I sat on the stone wall in the front garden for a few minutes then I got in the car.

What would I find when I went in? Him touching her? Playing with her hair the way he does? Telling her all the right things?

I'd had bad dreams that Chas wasn't real, that he told loads of women the same stuff he told me. After all, how could he be real? How could that floatation tank feeling he gave me be real? That feeling of being constantly surprised and interested by what he had to say? Of being so proud to show him off to my friends and colleagues? Of lying on him in bed, nuzzling into the perfect amount of hair on his chest? He was too good to be real . . . I needed him back . . . I was going to go in. But first, before going in to beg with heart-felt speech using eloquent prose including some of the above, I tried to look in through a teeny window just to check he was there (liar! I peered to check if *she* was there).

I couldn't see him, so I went around to the other side of the building. I jumped up, but the window there was too high, so I found a crate and stood on it, then looked down through the window and into the small kitchen. I couldn't see anything, but I could hear Chas on the other side . . .

'. . . You are my best friend, my light . . .'

My gasp caused me to fall from the crate.

When I got up I could hear whispering and giggling in the toilet. I ducked as quickly as I could and listened . . . to a kiss noise.

Kiss kiss noise.

Mmm, from her.

Mmm, her again.

I fell off the crate again and bashed my forehead. Furiousness fired me all the way back to Mum's. This Madeleine was his best friend, his light . . . she had a job he understood, one that didn't make her drink when she was stressed, who was relaxed and safe; she'd probably had orgasms all her life, without batteries, and she had no children to complicate matters.

I drove back to Mum and Dad's house and lied to them.

'He wasn't there,' I said to Mum. 'I need to get to work.'

I kissed Robbie goodbye as Mum tried to apologise for the punch, which she hadn't actually meant to do. Had my nose grown? Did she need glasses? She was so sorry, but so glad I'd sorted it out.

'Good,' I said.

I did very little at work. I was furious all day.

And that night, after collecting Robbie and putting him to bed, I reverted to the Laura Plan of break-up management, whereby the chuckee submerges him or herself in unrelated business such as chickens or murder investigations.

I sat on the window sill with my wine and my cigarette, cigarette, cigarette, and after the tenth cigarette (fourth wine) I quietly retrieved the blackboard from Robbie's room and placed it by the window so as to not stub my toe the next morning and looked at the columns I had drawn the previous evening. I would do this methodically, because that is how Ms Foster would do it (I could see my reflection in the kitchen window and it was uncanny, the likeness), one suspect at a time, and the first column was Jeremy, but I knew what there was to know about him, so I would begin with the second column, which was Mr and Mrs Kelly.

FORTY-ONE

MR AND MRS KELLY . . . Jealous? Betrayed? Bitter?
Angry? Torn? Worried? I'd written this on the blackboard the
evening before and had decided to check them out for myself.
I've never stopped being surprised by how much people are
willing to tell social workers. You can sit down with someone and ask them without any foreplay if they want to kill
themselves, if they have Hep C, if their father beat them, if
they were sexually abused by a neighbour, if the house they
lived in had a landline and a satellite dish, and they will tell
you, mostly, unless they have enough money and arrogance
to be unused to rude prying thirty-five-year-olds taking smug
judgemental notes about them.

I discovered that Mr and Mrs Kelly had neither money nor
arrogance. Mr Kelly had worked in construction. Mrs Kelly
had been a part-time dinner lady. The people in their neighbourhood were used to social workers knocking at doors
and asking things like this:

How's Amanda getting on?

I've been doing Jeremy's pre-trial report, and I was just
worried about Amanda.

How are you?

How did it feel when you found out she'd tracked Bridget
down?

You didn't know she'd found Bridget?

How did that feel?

Oh, you have a satellite dish!

Let me know, won't you, if there's anything I can do. And
thanks.

Hmm, I thought in my smug judgemental way as I drove back to the office. Hmm.

They were ordinary people, Mr and Mrs Kelly. They lived in a shoebox and shopped in bulk. They said they didn't know anything about the reunion of mother and daughter till after she was murdered, which is why they'd never been questioned. But what if they were lying? What if they'd found out and watched the love of their life run off to another? Watched the person they'd devoted themselves to never settle because they were never enough? It'd drive a person mad, drive them to Crinan with kitchen knives.

There was nothing on the system about them, and no previous convictions according to Bond, so I did some proper work for a change while Danny ignored me in his blind inimitable way.

After work, I struggled through my new single mother routine. Collect son, thank parents, pretend to be happy, check messages from Chas (none), play, cook, clean, do washing, bath, story, pretend to be happy, put Robbie to bed.

Drink and smoke.

'Krissie! It's ten to ten o'clock at night. I'm in bed!' Amanda said. 'What the fuck are you doing, investigating shit like this? How dare you? My mum and dad would never do anything bad! Do you hear me? Stay out of this, I'm fucked off with you. They didn't even know I'd found her! Oh, and they were at church. Ask Aunty Jean and Uncle Brian. No don't. Just stay out of this for Christ's sake.'

All right. All right. So they were nice, none-the-wiser and at church with a hundred people. I crossed the second column from my board and moved on to the next.

FORTY-TWO

'HAMISH McGIVERN', I had written on my blackboard. 'Employed, married . . .' Then this girl comes along, I pondered, and churns everything up.

He was a teacher, Amanda had told me. A burnt-out chemistry teacher in a posh private school outside Stirling. He spent his weekends with mates, and his weeks working towards the grades the school insisted on. An okay life, but maybe just okay.

'He was playing golf,' Amanda said, when I rang her at 11 p.m. to talk to her about Hamish. 'There are four men who testify to it. He wouldn't have done it. He's a good guy, and he loved her, and you have to stop. You're going crazy. Please don't call me again.'

Did he love her? Could he, when tragedy marked the beginning for them, and the end? Did he love that she closed her eyes sometimes and imagined him different?

Okay, I thought to myself, he was playing golf, and that was that. As much as he might have wanted to, he hadn't. I crossed him off, had a ciggie and one last wee drop, and then I began to wonder . . . Amanda. Why was she so defensive? So odd? Why would she want me to stop helping? Why would she get angry when the love of her life could be behind bars for life? Laughing when she shouldn't be laughing. Telling me all about Jeremy killing Bella in our second interview, to plant it. Not telling the police about the affair. Not trying hard enough to persuade Jeremy's mother to tell the truth about his whereabouts. Had she tried at all? She never said she had.

She'd thought of nothing else all her life. Wanted this person, this great Disneyland that was hers but not hers, dreamt of the meeting, of the special understandings, of the shared sorrow and emptiness, and then she finds her, and it's not good. In fact it's disturbing. Is it?

Even though genetic sexual attraction seemed to be quite common, the more I thought about it on the window sill that night, the more I doubted Amanda.

Had she harboured resentment against her mother since discovering she was adopted? Had she always wanted revenge? Had she planned it all? The sexual relationship, the murder?

'The Amanda complex', I wrote under her name on the blackboard. I stared at it for a while, then underlined it deliberately with my red chalk. As I did this one of my freshly tended nails broke, which was annoying at first, and then, as I bit the rest off, it hit me.

FORTY-THREE

After leaving Robbie with Mum and Dad, I dropped by Amanda's salon on the way to work.

'Oh God,' she sighed. 'What now?'

'Nothing. I want to apologise,' I said, checking to see where she had left her brown leather manicure set. It was on her wee table.

'Fine,' said Amanda, turning to escort me to the door. With her back in front of me, I grabbed the manicure set from her table and hid it in my bag.

'Sorry, Amanda,' I said, heading out the door she held open. 'I'll try not to bother you again.'

A few minutes later I ran into an office, where Jeremy's solicitor, sat at his ostentatious desk sipping very good coffee.

I thumped the manicure set on the desk.

'Put a glove on!' I said, and he did, before unzipping it.

'Toe clippers?'

'And all sorts of nail equipment. Amanda does it for a living, and she used this particular set on her nearest and dearest.'

'I'm not following.'

'The DNA! She did Jeremy's nails on the sofa all the time, and she told me she did Bridget's that weekend. That might be why Jeremy's DNA is under Bridget's nails.'

The solicitor looked up at me. 'Maybe, but it's a long shot.'

I drove wildly to the prison, secret agent style. My heart was thumping with excitement, but I wanted to keep my cool, get

as much information as I could from as many sources as possible. Most importantly, I didn't want to get his hopes up,
not yet.

As I walked past the first few interview rooms, I spotted
James Marney. He was in with the prison housing officer,
who gestured for me to come in.

'How are you?' I asked, desperate to get out of there as
fast as possible, to see Jeremy.

'The police have okayed a flat in the Gorbals,' said the
housing officer, a woman too young and too pretty to work
in a prison. 'And Mr Marney wanted to say something to
you, didn't you James?'

Oh God, I fidgeted. There'd be no getting away for a few
minutes at least. I had to sit down and listen to the guy.

'I'm sorry about Mum and Dad's,' he said, his hands shaking so hard he clutched the side of the desk to try and stop
them. 'I love my kids more than anything. They've already
lost their mum. I just don't want them to lose their dad as
well. I've told my parents I did do it.'

'And what did you do, Mr Marney?' I wanted to hear him
say it.

'I masturbated to pornography in front of them and made
them touch me on the penis, first James junior, then little
Robert.'

I coughed. Oh God.

He gulped, looking almost as ill as I felt. 'My parents
understand now that I can't see them without supervision.
Please don't make me live my life without them.'

He went on and on. Apologetic, remorseful, willing to co-
operate with anything so he could see them, desperate to try
to make amends for the terrible offences he'd committed
against them.

I told him I'd get in touch with the relevant authorities to
see if supervised access might be possible. I didn't shake his
hand, but I have to admit I felt a bit sorry for him as I left

the room. His mouth had been so dry while he spoke it had made an awful clicking noise.

'I'll see you in the next couple of days, okay?' I said, leaving the room to talk to Jeremy, who was ready and waiting two doors down.

'Jeremy, I want to talk to you about Amanda,' I said. We sat in the same positions as last time, and by now all thoughts of him being a murderer were gone. He was broken, sadness oozed from every section of him, and I gave him a soft smile that was not a social worker smile, but the smile of a friend.

'Aren't you angry with her?' I asked him. 'For not telling them about the . . . affair? It could have changed things?'

He was silent for a moment, and then he said it very quietly.

'I am angry, but not because she hasn't got me out of here. That's up to the lawyers. But she kissed her own mother, slept with her own mother. How can I get my head around that? I can't. But you know, Krissie, it's the betrayal that makes me angry most of all. I thought she was mine. I thought we were forever.'

Once, when I was tiny, I felt this kind of connection with someone: the same thoughts, the same feelings, at the same time as me. It was my friend Sarah, we were only wee, and it only happened for the briefest of times, but I still remembered it. Sarah, the beautiful friend I'd lost two years back. The words that had come from her mouth as we played with her doll in my garden had been my words, as were Jeremy's now, and I felt right into him, and he into me.

Shit, I was crying. I was apologising and telling him that Chas had left me. I was sitting with a remand prisoner in Sandhill crying, and before I knew it Jeremy was holding my hand and looking into my eyes and saying thank you, thank you, for being the only one he could talk to, be with.

'And don't worry about Billy Mullen,' he said. 'That's all

sorted out now. Just hold on to the stuff for a while and I'll let you know what to do with it.'

And when I finally stopped my tears, he added, 'But I do wonder why no one saw her on that train.'

'Sorry?'

'Amanda. She drops off her hire car in Oban and then gets the train to Glasgow. She does this four-hour trip, walks home, and no one sees her. It's just strange.'

FORTY-FOUR

Amanda Amanda Amanda Amanda, I thought as I drove back to work.

She'd done it.

She'd sought out the woman who abandoned her, angry. Seduced her, took her to the hills and killed her. She'd even managed to set up her poor husband, transferring his nail gunk from the manicure tools to Bridget's nails.

By the time I found a park outside my building, I had devised a very clever plan. I was going to use an unorthodox ingenious method that may one day be labelled the Donald Technique.

But not yet. The office was buzzing with emergencies. I started to realise criminal justice social work was easily as stressful as child care. Deadlines and angry men weighed on me constantly. I rarely saw my colleagues, or my boss. New cases and new reports appeared in my pigeonhole each morning and I fumbled through each day the best I could.

After an afternoon of such fumbling, I walked into the Pine Tree Unisex Hairdressing Salon to confront Amanda.

'Did you kill Bridget?'

This was my ploy, an underused one I considered: to get to know the suspect very well, then look them directly in the eye and ask them.

Unfortunately, Amanda had just sipped an over-boiled Costa latte, which sprayed me in the face and really hurt.

'Get out! Get the fuck out of here!'

Her boss joined in. 'You're crazy! Get out!'

I backed out of the salon, Amanda following me angrily.

'Do you know what happened to her?' she yelled as I retreated, embarrassed and ashamed, to my car.

'It was a fucking monster.' Amanda's voice began to soften. She leant against the window of the salon and slid down it, crying. 'A monster.'

All right, I thought, squatting down beside her, my hand on her shoulder. So maybe she didn't do it, and maybe she'd already gone through all this with the police, but why had no one seen her on the train?

'Why did no one see you on the train?' I asked (unable to let go of the ridiculous Donald Technique idea above).

'I told you,' she said, blowing her nose. 'I cried in the loo the entire time.'

'But you bought a ticket?'

'There was no one at the station, and like I said, I sat in the loo. I didn't not buy one deliberately; I just couldn't get myself out of that space.'

'But you did eventually, at Central station.'

'Of course.'

'Well, someone must have seen you, going home, or when you got there?'

'Why am I fucking talking to you?' She flicked my hand from her shoulder and stood up, angry again. 'Why won't you go away? I was distraught. I walked home, snuck in the back door, and slept all day. Well, I didn't sleep, I lay there and cried.'

'I'm sorry for upsetting you,' I said, standing up. 'I know I'm a bit weird. I just want to be logical. I want to help Jeremy.'

'Why are you so interested in Jeremy? Why are you spending so much time asking me questions when you should be trying to fix your own life?'

'CCTV,' I said. One of my probationers had been done for police assault in Central Station. Swore blind he didn't do it, till he saw himself on camera kicking the plain-clothed cop in the head, four times. 'Did they check for you?'

'No, because I'm not a fucking suspect. You're the only idiot who seems to think I am.'

'Just a little favour?' I said to Bond, whose direct line I was phoning yet again, and I realised that I was getting the hang of this job, that this was the way it worked. Be nice to people, get their numbers, talk, tell them stuff, the more information the better. It could really come in handy, and it had, because now he was going to do something for me.

'You shouldn't be asking me this,' he said.

'I can bring biscuits,' I begged.

'Ice cream,' he said, so I made my way over to the station via the Derby Café.

We hadn't finished our oyster wafers with raspberry sauce when she came out of the 0830 from Oban clear as day. Red eyes, forlorn and exhausted, dragging her small backpack alongside her and slipping past the turnstile while the ticket inspectors were looking the other way.

'She didn't pay!' said Bond.

'So nail the bitch!' I said, tossing the remains of my ice cream into the bin.

I felt bad when I rang Amanda. She had been my friend, as much as I knew she shouldn't have been, and yet I had suspected her. But not any more. She was already on the train when Bridget died at 0900.

'I know I was on the fucking train,' Amanda said, and hung up.

On the way home, I dropped in on Mrs Bagshaw. She let me in, and returned to the half-smoked cigarette on the table. At least fifty butts indicated she'd been sitting in that position for some time, looking at the river, waiting.

'Have one,' she said, and over the next hour I realised that this was a woman who had both dosh and arrogance, who did not answer questions just because they were asked. She told me nothing. She didn't know Amanda, had only met her once, hadn't seen her in Glasgow because she'd wanted it that way, a secret. Yes, that's Bella, in the garden at Oxford. She'd be twenty-four tomorrow.

I'd come to beg her to tell the truth about Jeremy's whereabouts on the night of the murder.

'He was with you, wasn't he?' I prompted.

Mrs Bagshaw was silent for a while, and then threw me a cold stare that made me shiver.

'I am almost ready to forgive him,' she said.

I couldn't get out of there fast enough.

FORTY-FIVE

I collected Robbie, went home, and soaked him in for a while. As he laughed at the video he was watching, I found myself marvelling at his simplicity, and praying that he would grow up to be happier than me.

I was desperately sad. I missed Chas. I wanted him. Where the hell was he?

With Robbie in bed, I couldn't help reaching for the bottle of wine that I couldn't help buying on the way home from work.

I wiped the blackboard clean and poured another glass. The Hamish column, the Kelly one, the Amanda one, the Jeremy one, then the Rachel one, which was the only column with nothing in it. I stopped myself. Rachel.

'Rachel McGivern,' I said to the duty social worker in Stirling first thing Monday morning. I'd had no sleep that weekend and no quality time with Robbie. It was a shit time, wishing Chas would phone me or turn up, putting my boy in front of too many videos while I drank either red wine or Soluble Anadin.

'She's eighteen, not sure of her birthday,' said the duty social worker.

'Oh aye, here she is . . .' She tapped on the computer. 'Not allocated, but there was a report once, to the children's hearing. Let me see. A fight with another girl. She was fifteen, had a knife, outside the school. There was no further action. The case was closed.'

'Could you fax me the report?' I asked.

'Sure.'

Everyone was in the office. Robert, who was reading out bits of the report he was writing . . .

'When asked if he had molested her on the train,' he read, 'Mr Jones replied that he had merely attempted to disembark . . . "I tried to get aff, but she was a fat bastard!" he informed the writer.'

Penny didn't laugh, being on the large and bastardy side herself.

But Danny did, and I saw this momentary lapse in shut-off-ness as an opportunity to apologise, at last.

'I am so sorry.'

'For what?'

'Interfering with you.'

'That's all right. Jesus, how much did you have?'

'A couple of bottles of this and that. I hadn't really had any for two years, shouldn't have. Do I have an alcohol problem, do you think? Am I one of the social work casualties?'

'If I said to you that you can't have one tonight would you feel panicky?'

'No.'

'Then you don't.'

'Yes.'

'Then you do.'

'I'm not going to have one tonight.'

'Good idea.'

I sighed, panicky already, and then walked to the fax machine.

On the way, I spotted the elusive Hilary, finally back at work. She was in her office, looking deadly serious as she spoke on the phone.

The report slid out of the fax machine and I devoured it in reception. Rachel McGivern, truant, offender. Ran away from home continually in early teens, mother reported drinking episodes and anger problems. Rachel herself argued simply that her mother didn't care, that she was obsessed with work and other things. The report concluded that it was attention-seeking behaviour, that there was enough openness, support and determination to resolve matters, and that statutory measures were not required.

Nothing new. Except that Rachel was always an angry, jealous girl who craved her mother's attention, who had carried an offensive weapon before, and who had a history of violence.

FORTY-SIX

I was a genius investigator. If investigating were my job, I would be promoted. I would be given a bigger car and a more powerful gun and an easily impressed partner. If investigating were my job.

It all became so clear. Rachel, the angry mother-hater, was more put out than anyone at the arrival of this new family member.

I did a risk assessment using assessment tools I'd not yet been trained in using – LSI-R, RA1-4, GUT-FEELING-313b – and it all added up. Rachel was at least at medium risk of violent re-offending, I reckoned – past history, alcohol abuse, suspected drug use, suspended from school twice, poor relationship with her mother, mates who'd been in court, unemployed . . . the list went on.

I rang the solicitor's office.

'Have you checked out Rachel McGivern?' I blurted. 'She has a history of violence.'

'Listen,' the lawyer said, excited. 'He's on the scraper, in the wee bit at the end. There's loads of him, and loads of her.'

Bingo.

'You are a genius!' the lawyer said. 'But that's not all. This morning, Mrs Bagshaw came through with it. She rang an hour ago. Said you convinced her.'

'Really?'

At this point I noticed that Danny, who had been listening to me with a worried look on his face, had been beckoned into Hilary's office.

'Aye,' said the solicitor. 'After she was discharged from

hospital, he spent all night and all morning at her house. Jeremy couldn't have killed her. He was four hundred miles away. I'll have him out by the end of the day . . . He's asked if you could collect him. I'll pass on your concerns about Rachel, but leave it to the police, eh?'

'What are you doing?' came a hard-as-nails voice. I looked up to find Hilary hovering over me angrily.

'Say goodbye,' she said with none of that feathery-soft jargon bullshit she'd used when we first met.

'Come to my office now.'

My face was burning as I walked past Danny, Penny and Robert and into Hilary's office. Hilary slammed the door behind us.

'Just had a nice chat with PC Wilkinson.'

'Bond?'

'Wilkinson. He mentioned you've been working as a private detective. And Danny tells me that was a defence lawyer on the phone just now.'

'I . . .' She didn't let me continue. She had lots to say, including the following: I was unprofessional, naïve, silly, making an idiot of myself, who did I think I was, she could investigate me for misconduct but she wasn't going to. What she was going to do instead was limit my caseload to road traffic offences for six months. Till I realised who I was and that it was not my place to play fucking homicide detective.

'But he was innocent. Because of me he's getting out.'

'It's not your job or your concern. You can get yourself into serious trouble crossing the line like you have. Tell me, why did you became a social worker, Krissie?'

'What?'

'Why did you do social work? You're a straight A student. First class honours degree in history. Why social work?'

'Why not?' was my response.

I knew what she was asking. Did I think I was too clever for the job? Was I using social work as some kind of therapy, as a quest for justice because some bastard had abused me and poor Sarah? I knew what she was asking because I'd heard the same questions banging around in my head sometimes. If I'm honest, the answer to both questions was yes.

'You have a lot to learn, Krissie,' said Hilary.

Blimey. Numbed the good news of Jeremy's release a bit. Not so much as a thank you for being a genius investigator, a saver of the universe, for rescuing Jeremy from ten years behind bars, from being beaten by large hairy men with scars and fists, for saving Amanda from a life without the love of her life.

'You're right. I'm sorry,' I said. 'But he's expecting me to collect him.'

'After that I have three court reports for you – all of them for driving with no insurance.'

When I sat down at my desk, Danny made a kind of apology. 'She asked me and I just told her I was worried about you. It's not your fault. You've had no training or support at all through this.'

'Don't worry about it.'

'Are you all right?' asked Penny kindly. 'Do you want a cup of tea?'

Farty woman. Posh huffy old bird. As she held out her hand to offer her support, I realised that she had the kindest eyes I've ever seen. If I was a client, it'd be her I'd want to talk to.

'I'd love one,' I said, and it was the most comforting cup of tea I've ever had.

When I phoned Amanda afterwards, she didn't swear at me for a change. She was excited, thankful and apologetic.

'Do you want a lift to the prison?' I asked her. 'I'll call as soon as we know what time they'll be letting him out.'

Next I phoned Mrs Bagshaw to ask her if she wanted me to take her too. She was as odd as ever. 'Yes, I told the police he was with me. I am ready to forgive him now. I've asked them not to tell him I confirmed his alibi, because I want to surprise him here, at the apartment. Don't tell him yet. Would you bring him here, Krissie? I've made his favourite meal – you remember? I can't face the prison, but I still want to surprise him.'

'I'll drop him off as soon as he's out,' I promised, shaking my head at her persistent weirdness.

I drove to Mum and Dad's for lunch. It's funny, when you have good or bad news, you need to tell everyone immediately, as if saying it over and over makes it real, somehow. But when I got to Mum and Dad's I realised that this news wasn't real to them, it had nothing to do with them, me either really, and so it became less exciting by the second.

'You need to make up with Chas,' Dad said over stew.

'I think he's with someone called Madeleine,' I said.

It was like taking home a trophy won gloriously, before crowds. I had helped Jeremy, helped Amanda, but now I was home and all I had was a bowl of stew. I was miserable.

Even Robbie looked miserable. 'Potion!' he said in between swear words, and I tried to mix flour with fairy liquid and be excited about it, but he could tell it wasn't really magic potion, wouldn't really give the fairies faster wings, that it was just soap and flour and very messy, and we both sighed at each other in Mum and Dad's kitchen and wished for two weeks ago.

Mum and Dad felt almost as bad. They loved Chas as much as they loved me, and him being with someone else hurt them the same. But they couldn't believe it – he was their boy, their lovely Chas, the best thing to have ever been in their daughter's life.

'Are you sure?' Mum asked.

'I keep seeing them together. Since the party, when I kissed Danny, he's been with her, putting roses in her hair, telling her she's his best friend and his light, and I heard them kissing.'

'Heard them kissing?' (Mum's moment of hope)

'And talking, too.'

'Oh.' (Dashed)

'Do you want to stay here tonight?'

'No, I need to go home. I need to put this lovely little boy to bed with a story and a cuddle and then I need to not have a glass of wine.'

I took a Nicorette inhaler out of my pocket – Danny had given it to me that morning as part of my action plan – and sucked hard on it.

'Looks like a tampon,' Mum said.

'I know.'

The solicitor still hadn't phoned when I got back to work after lunch. He was in court. I left him a message with my home number, tore up Jeremy's report, sent another one to court that I'd somehow managed to complete in forty minutes, and left to get money out of my dwindling bank account and buy a present for Jeremy and Amanda – a silver quaich.

When I nipped home to wrap the present, I noticed that Chas had been there. He'd left the step ladder in the wrong place, and a note on the kitchen table – 'Can you please call me?'

I dialled his number immediately, my heart racing. But it rang out, so I left a message. Fuck.

I sniffed out other hints of Chas. His favourite jeans and T-shirt gone, a photo of Robbie moved slightly to the left, toothbrush and shaving cream gone, the kitchen window left open. He'd had a glass of water and left it in the sink, looked through the mail and taken a bank statement and a letter from the art gallery. Then he'd written the note, closed both sets of doors and left.

Another thing I noticed on the way out was the wedding dress I'd bought.

It was hanging on the back of the bedroom door. I touched the bodice, the Nutella stain still alive and well, and found myself kissing my hand and then it, that soft white thing that was the future I'd probably lost.

The phone rang. It was the solicitor. Jeremy was being released. He was waiting for me to come and get him.

'Good thing you did Jeremy's nails,' I said to Amanda, after picking her up en route to the prison.

'I looked for that manicure set for hours,' she replied. 'Glad you stole it, though.'

I thought of the things Chas and I did together. Chas grew fly-legs from his nose, and I would gather them between my two fingers, yank and then count the number of black nose hairs on my fingertip. We even did this as a party trick to freak people out. (The best was fifteen.)

Then there was the tiny gap between my two front teeth, that I could squirt water out of by pressing my tongue hard against it. I would often catch Chas's eyeball unaware from impressive distances. Oh, and there was the time he used his razor to make me Brazilian and all the times he used mine to make his face smooth. When I thought about it, Chas's DNA was everywhere on me still, and mine on him, but that was all we had of each other, just flakes of dead cells.

Was it another life? Would I be able to return to the realm of the loved, take a cup of coffee in bed, be parents together with Chas, cook meals in on Friday nights and read stories together beside a chubby smiley little curly-haired boy?

FORTY-SEVEN

Amanda was about to re-enter *her* previous life, the one where she was married to a successful property developer and living in a lovely flat in Islington and showing off to the friends she'd left in Glasgow. She'd missed him, but missing him had been overshadowed by the events following the wedding party in Glasgow.

Finding Bridget.

Feeling things she hadn't known know how to express.

Expressing them in a way that made her feel confused and guilty.

And Bridget's brutal death, a constant nightmare, in her unconsciousness and consciousness.

Then Jeremy's arrest. The man she loved. How could anyone think he could do such a thing?

As Krissie's car neared Sandhill prison, Amanda's heart beat fast with excitement and nerves. Would Jeremy have changed after his experiences in prison? Would he blame her? Would he cope with her grief? With the fact that she sometimes cried all day, and sometimes all night, and hardly slept or ate?

Would Jeremy still love her? Would he love her if he knew that jumping naked onto beds was the last thing she felt like doing?

She was nervous, but she believed he would. He was her Jeremy. The man she had fallen in love with that night in the Earls Court hostel, who had forgiven her that day in the police cell when she told him about what happened with

Bridget, who was a poor vulnerable soul who needed the love he'd been denied from the age of four.

She spent all day preparing for him. Hair and skin and clothes and perfume. She made the bedroom welcoming and comfortable, bought chocolate she knew he liked, and prayed. Dear God, please let this be the end of it. Please let us be as happy as we can, and please let Bridget be in heaven. Amen.

The horn beeped. It was the weirdo social worker who seemed to have nothing better to do than ferry her around and talk non-stop about Jeremy. Why the fuck were taxpayers paying for people to have manicures and drive people around like that? It was scandalous, and something worth taking to her local MP once she got a lift to the prison because she didn't have a car.

Oh God, she was nervous. In an hour she would hold him, take him home. They would be together. She would ask him to move to Scotland and he would say yes, and they would begin a family. A boy and a girl. Or two girls and a boy, three . . . Charlie, Rachel and Anna. She was smiling, despite the nerves, as she got into Krissie's car to find a present on the passenger seat, and her smile subsided as she wondered what the taxpayers would say if they knew they'd just paid for a useless wedding gift.

FORTY-EIGHT

Overjoyed at the news of his release, Jeremy walked towards the confessional again. Father Moscardini had become a friend, or at least a trustworthy confidant, and he liked him. He wasn't patronising or mean, didn't call him a 'body' or call lunch 'feeding time'. He treated him like a human being.

The last time Jeremy had seen the priest was a week ago at lunch time. It had been Friday, which meant the 'lucky bucket'. This extra menu item excited the men in C hall beyond belief, that they could have more food than the usual hospital portions – but a bucket of the week's leftovers – baked beans and fish fingers and hamburgers and chips and rice and curry, all mixed to warm mush in a prison cauldron – did not excite Jeremy at all. In fact it made him feel sick. Jeremy took a roll instead, and the priest smiled at him with understanding.

'How are you feeling?' asked Father Moscardini.

'Good,' Jeremy had lied, and the priest followed him to his cell.

He'd had the cell to himself since his last co-pilot moved onwards and upwards to the convicted hall, and he'd been feeling scared. If he got out, how would he cope? What would happen next? Father Moscardini talked to him for hours, first about music and sport, then travelling and then love.

'From what you've said over the past few weeks,' said the priest, 'you seem like a romantic. You love with every piece of you, give with every piece of you, and there is nothing wrong with that. You will get over this terrible time, but first you must get over what happened to you when you were a tiny boy. Come to confession again. Don't be scared off this time.'

'It does scare me,' Jeremy said. 'I'll think about it.'

That was a week ago. He was free now, about to face life head-on, and he knew he couldn't leave those prison walls without seeing Father Moscardini once more.

FORTY-NINE

I want to get one thing straight. I never led Jeremy on.

After Amanda and I went to see him at Sandhill that afternoon, I went over each of my interviews in great detail and I'm absolutely sure I never led him on.

The first time I saw him, when I arrived fresh with my report request, he'd told me about London, about him and Amanda meeting in the bar, moving in together, then deciding to get married. He'd told me about Bella. I'd told him about Chas, for rapport. (Shit, over-share – mental note not to disclose personal information to clients again.) But if anything, I told myself later that evening, this information would have made it clear I was out of bounds.

The second interview, when he'd just been beaten. It had been the 'You-can-tell-me' interview. Nothing untoward.

The third, when he told me he was in danger, that we were both in danger.

Then in the suicide cell, after he'd tried to hang himself, I'd watched, mainly, as he and Amanda hugged in the corner.

The next time I saw him, I told him about the drugs and Billy, and how my little boy was in danger.

The sixth and last was when I told him Chas had left me.

Shite, I'd seen the guy six times for a report that required one half-hour interview. And I'd over-shared to buggery, something I'd never do again. Still, I had never ever led Jeremy to believe I wanted to be with him romantically, or that I was his best girl.

'My best girl!' he'd said after I walked into the Sandhill's reception area.

I'd left Amanda in the foyer and asked Bob, the prison social worker, to leave his crossword for a bit and take me through to the reception area, where Jeremy was waiting to be escorted into freedom.

The reception area was a Portakabin filled with cubicles like those around old swimming pools, where men changed into either freedom or the opposite. Ten men were waiting with uncontainable grins, their belongings in hand, good intentions in head – though many of these good intentions would dissolve at the off licence in Lee Street.

Jeremy didn't have the huge optimistic grin of his colleagues. He was standing in casual clothes, looking rather gorgeous actually, and the bruises and cuts on his face had died down.

He touched my arm and smiled. 'Thank you, Krissie. You've saved me.'

He looked different, very different. Suddenly taller, straighter, with equal eyes.

'I've been to confession,' he said.

'Excellent!' I said, and hugged him. After all, he was no longer a criminal. No longer my client.

'Amanda's waiting in the foyer. But before I go get her, tell me what I should do with the drugs, Jeremy. I don't want to get you into trouble.'

He ignored my question. 'I don't want to see her.'

I thought he'd be desperate, that he'd run to her and I'd watch the product of my hard work, twirling around and kissing through the smiles.

'But why? She's so excited,' I said, my surprise momentarily drowning out the drugs in my kitchen.

He leaned in towards me. 'She slept with her mother.'

'I know that. But it wasn't exactly . . .'

'I've had so much time to think, and I wanted to forgive her, but I can't.'

'Jeremy, you have to talk to her and sort things out. It's been a terrible time, but . . .'

'I just feel so mixed up,' he interrupted. 'But you're right, I have to talk to her. Will you do me a favour?' he asked

'Of course.'

'Sit with me, while I talk to Amanda? It could be difficult. We might need you.'

A front row seat to tragedies in progress. That's my job, to sit with salty popcorn and watch – this time Jeremy breaking Amanda's heart in a small room in the special visits area of Sandhill.

There was silence for a moment as she hugged him, but then he pulled back his face, suddenly grave.

'I can't be with you Amanda.'

Amanda's face compartmentalised into sections of brokenness.

'So much has happened. And I probably could have coped, if not for what you did, with Bridget I mean. I don't think I'll ever be able to get through it. We were on honeymoon! But that's not the main thing, in the end.'

Amanda looked shell-shocked. 'What *is* the main thing?' she asked.

'The main thing is that I've fallen in love with someone else.'

'What?'

I think we both asked this question at the same time, wondering who on earth he could have fallen for in prison – Chuggy from C hall? Father Moscardini in Chaplaincy?

As the silence dragged on, both sets of eyes turned to me, and I realised what he was going to say as he said it.

'Krissie. I'm in love with you, Krissie.'

Of course I told him it was ridiculous. 'Jeremy! What are you talking about?' I said.

He went bright red.

'I'm sorry if I've given the wrong impression!'

Amanda ran out of the room, and I wasn't sure what to do next.

'Jeremy, you're a good man, and I can understand you feel some kind of . . . gratitude, but . . .'

'I'm sorry,' he said. 'I feel like an idiot.'

'It's all right. But it's goodbye now, Jeremy. I'm a social worker. I've crossed the line and I've become over-involved. In the process I've screwed my life up. But you know what, I'm going to fix things. I'm going to get Chas back. He's the only one for me, always has been. I did your report, that's all.' I shook his hand. 'Goodbye, Jeremy. I need to go.'

'Of course. My God, I'm such an idiot. Goodbye, Krissie. I'm sorry.'

I raced out to get Amanda, but she had gone. Her taxi was screeching down the driveway as I exited the revolving doors.

As the doors slowed behind me, whirling people in and out of the big hoose, I took a huge breath. Suddenly, rays of light pierced through the sky as if to say: 'It's over now, Krissie. You're out of the water. You can take a breath. Go!'

FIFTY

Amanda somehow found her way home. She fell into the hall and her mother caught her. 'Oh, my darling,' she said, holding her tight on the couch as her dad raced in from the garden. 'It's okay, my love. It's okay. We're here. We're here.'

He'd gone. Just as Bridget had.

And what was left?

Her mother, her beautiful mother, holding her tight and telling her she'd be all right.

Her father, her kind-hearted father, doing the same.

She would stay in that house, on that sofa, for a long time. She would be fed and held and watched for a long long time, and after a while, the sick feeling in her tummy would fade and she would start to feel good, maybe even one day wonderful. And maybe, for the first time since that dinner at the age of six, when her folks decided she was old enough to know where she came from, she would realise that she'd always known where she came from, that there was nothing else to wonder, nothing else to find and nowhere else to go.

But once a year, on the anniversary of Bridget's death, she would go shopping. She would take her time, choosing the most beautiful card she could find. She would tremble as she sat in the restaurant in Bridge of Allan where she and Bridget had shared three bottles of wine together.

From your wee ginger nut, she would write, before sealing it with tears, adding no address and popping it in the post

FIFTY-ONE

As I drove home from Sandhill I became more and more determined not to let a wire-ball girl ruin my life with Chas. So maybe they'd been shopping together, maybe they'd kissed, but Chas and I were meant for each other. No amount of shopping and kissing would destroy us.

He'd been working towards the biggest event in his career. His opening. He'd been painting for years, and had finally been given the chance, and I had not only been a bastard but had also completely forgotten that the opening was tonight.

Everything had sun shining on it. Robbie's smile when I went to pick him up, Mum and Dad's garden, the Clyde as I drove home with my mission to get Chas back, the flat with those gorgeous hardwood floors and my wardrobe filled with flattering outfits.

I bathed Robbie, dressed him in his Hunting Donald kilt and chose an outfit. I remembered I had one thing to clear out of my life before heading to the gallery to get my old one back. No more hiding things away, ignoring things in the hope that time and silence would fix them. I would tell this Madeleine to get the fuck away from my man. I was so excited. I would beg, apologise, make promises, not talk too much, kiss him, hug him, touch him, not drink, look at the paintings I had never been allowed to look at.

But first.

I tripped over the small stepladder that had been left in the middle of the kitchen and swore at it. Why had Chas moved it that morning? I opened it out and stood on it. I reached up above the pelmet at the top, to the dusty ceiling of the wall unit, and felt the plastic box where I had hidden two cigarette packets filled with class A drugs a few days earlier, packets that I would take to the police before going to the opening. I pulled the box down with me and looked into it.

There was nothing there.

FIFTY-TWO

Chas had been to the flat earlier that day. He'd had enough of the silliness. Days of not talking to his soul mate, and for what? Some daft attempt to get him jealous? The photo was laughable – Danny uncomfortable and trying to get away, Krissie looking out of the side of her eyes to see if Chas was looking. He hadn't worried about that for a moment. But her volatile behaviour had been driving him bonkers. And he had an exhibition to get ready for. He couldn't afford to fuck it up.

A few days out, he'd decided, would be best for both of them. Because despite his mostly un-macho attributes, Chas felt the desperate need to provide for his new family. He'd travelled and wasted time for too long. He'd also decided he wanted to get married. Soon as he saw her in that over-the-top dress that was still hanging in the bedroom, waiting, he knew. She looked glorious, a white fluffy bride, and he would marry her.

He would, he decided, propose to her at the party. He day-dreamed about having children with her. A house with a garden, without four flights of steps and nosy noisy neighbours. He wanted to take his family to Rome for the week-end, or spend the summer somewhere with sun and language. He wanted to be settled. Boring, settled family life was what he wanted, and that meant he had to make money. And if he couldn't make money painting, he was going to need to find another way.

He smelt the smoke and opened the window with a sigh. Krissie had given up years ago. What the hell was she doing?

He knew where her stash was, took the stepladder out, stood on it, and reached up above the wall unit. He was surprised to find the photos in the container – of the speed and the dope. He was also surprised to find the threatening letter, from his friend Billy. But mostly, he was surprised to find two cigarette packets filled with white powder.

Fuck, what had she been going through? How could he have been so selfish as to not realise, and not help her? He shook his head and then raced to Billy's house.

If Chas hadn't done that, hadn't taken things into his own hands and raced to Billy's house, then he would have been okay. He probably would have made it to the opening.

FIFTY-THREE

Robbie and I arrived at the gallery, which was overflowing.

In my self-obsession, I hadn't realised how big it was going to be.

Chas had been given the entire space to himself. There were posters at the front, with his honest face half-smiling to the world. His parents were there, my parents were there, and most of the people who'd witnessed me making an idiot of myself at the party were there, and I did a quick round of begging apologies before Robbie yelled 'Daddy!', pointing to the poster in the foyer. He then dragged me into the exhibition, three interconnecting white rooms, beautifully lit and filled with canvases.

I sat down on a seat in the middle, unable to stand, and just stared at the paintings.

Danny was sitting there too, and we were both silent as we took in the atmosphere.

Robbie, running from one red-stickered painting to the next, saying: 'Mummy, look! Mummy's peeking out behind that big rock . . . Mummy! Mummy you're floating in that dark sea. Mummy, look you're on a cloud! And in those triangles, the snow, the leaves, that big glass tower! Mummy, you're everywhere! Look!'

People were walking from canvas to canvas, not talking, and standing for a long time at each point. They were beautiful, his paintings from around the world, from the years he'd travelled without me. Nepal, India, New York, Australia, New Zealand, Vietnam. Every one of them was recognisable, and I was in every one of them.

'Do you want me to describe them to you?' someone asked Danny.

'No thanks,' I said for him. 'He gets it.'

I saw the wire-ball girl in the corner, and walked over to her nervously.

'I want to apologise to you,' I said. 'I've been a total bitch. But I love Chas and I'm not going to let you get in between us.'

'Fuck's sake,' said Madeleine. 'We're just mates, dick-wad. And you were rat-arsed. It's okay. But where's Chas?'

'Is he not here?'

'No. It's all happening in an hour. The celebrant's waiting and why aren't you dressed?' An attractive woman joined us and took hold of Madeleine's hand.

'Are you?' I began.

'*Lesbians* . . .' Madeleine said sarcastically. 'Better not get too close!'

I realised that it was these two I'd heard kissing in the toilet as I'd listened from my plastic crate outside the studio. I looked at their hands, comfortable and affectionate. God, I was a fuckwit of the first order.

'Celebrant?' I asked.

'Have you not seen Chas today?' Madeleine asked me.

'No.'

'But . . . Shit,' she said. 'Shit.' They looked at each other, then at me, their eyes wide with worry, and then told me. Chas had gone home that afternoon to propose to me. Plan A had been to propose at the party, but I'd scuppered that one with drug-induced psychosis and alcoholism. So he was going to do it at the flat when I arrived home from work – the whole caboodle: down on one knee, ring, speech, the lot. He'd practised it, over and over . . .

'You are my best friend. My light . . .' I said, remembering what I'd overheard Chas say to Madeleine at the studio.

He'd arranged for us to be married after the opening, she told me. He knew it was the only way I'd cope with the stress of it, if he surprised me. He'd filled in forms and worked like a dog.

I looked around and noticed a fat woman with a book smiling at me. The celebrant. I noticed the spectacular food on the tables in the empty room next door, the set tables and chairs, and oh my God, he'd done everything, and he'd gone to get me that morning, and something had gone horribly wrong.

Because he hadn't made it.

I remembered tripping over the ladder in the kitchen and I realised. Chas had found the drugs, and the photos. And Chas, being Chas, would have headed straight for Billy.

'Shit, he'll have gone to get Billy Mullen,' I said.

'Billy Mullen?' Danny repeated, having overheard our conversation. 'You mean the guy who was at your party?'

'Yeah, he took photos of me, threatened me.'

'Really?'

'He's a nutcase. I think he might kill Chas. I think he raped Jeremy and put him in hospital.'

'Krissie, I didn't want to say at the party, but I know Billy,' Danny said. 'He came into the office the day after he got out. They gave him probation, and a drug treatment and testing order. He's about six stone, Krissie, a skelf. I've seen him at his home every day this week.'

'So you know where he lives?'

'Aye, but listen to me. You've got it all wrong. This guy, Billy, he's lovely. Just addicted, that's all. I've had him before, know his family well. He's a good person.'

'How can you say that? He threatened my son. He tried to kill Jeremy. I think he even raped him.'

Danny took Krissie's hand and held it. 'Billy told me something bad happened in his cell at Sandhill . . .'

A beat.

'. . . But you've got it all wrong. I think it may have been the other way around.'

FIFTY-FOUR

It was very much the other way around.

Billy had been there that first time, after the banana incident, when the mad-psycho C hall rapist had taken Jeremy in his cell; ripped his jeans to the floor with the nod of a pervert officer yonder, and loosened him with polyunsaturated.

Billy hadn't wanted to be there. He'd cowered on his top bunk, looking down towards the poor fellow on the concrete, his face pushed hard into the cold floor. He let his Sandhill tough-nut guard down for a second, caught the poor guy's eyes to show sympathy, to ask forgiveness for not doing anything, and what he saw scared him more than the prospect of being next.

Jeremy was smiling.

When Mad-Psycho was done, Jeremy scraped himself from the ground and asked the thug if he was finished. He then head-butted the brute directly in the forehead, punched him seven or eight times in the nose, hard and fast, one, two, three, and so on, kicked his groin, and flung the limp man over the bottom bunk. Jeremy then pulled the man's head back by the hair, and pushed himself inside. Billy's top bunk banged against the wall with the seven or eight thrusts it took for Jeremy to come, and as the final drive was driven, Jeremy's knees trembled . . .

'Next time ahhh . . . sk,' he said before he kicked the flaccid man out of the cell to seek medical attention, and looked at Billy, who was shivering like a child on his little top bunk.

The incident had been successful for Jeremy in many

respects. Gave him status, and an idea of how to make her his.

Initially, he had it all sussed in prison. Had expensive dodgy lawyers working on his guilt-ridden mother for the alibi. So all he had to do was wait. He knew he'd be out soon, knew that the bitch would get it one way or the other.

Then Krissie came along and he realised it would be a good idea to work towards a heart-wrenching report, just in case. So he told her of suicide and unloving parents, and oh shit, here we go again, he said to himself in his cell after meeting her that first time, thinking hard about her tight little bottom and those perfect white teeth. Here we go again. He always fell in love too easily, always loved too hard. He found out exactly who her boyfriend was, where they lived, and how he might go about getting her trust and affection. He was a great businessman, Jeremy, and he knew that the best way to get someone to like you is to get them to do you a favour.

Billy did as Jeremy told him while he was in prison . . . Don't move or I'll slice your face with this carefully fash-ioned razor-bladed toothbrush . . . Get her to bring it in or I'll smash your head like this . . .

The 'Glasgow kisses' that smashed Billy's nose and fore-head and chin hurt.

Even more, the angry digits that prodded him in the middle of the night.

And, just in case Billy had decided against the plan, Jeremy rang him once a day after he was released, with the same advice . . . Do it, and the money is yours, all £30,000 of it . . . All you need is my pin number and you'll be sniffing cocaine so hard you'll cause a tsunami. No one will get hurt, your friends will be fine, but do it, or Rab here will pay you a visit after court tomorrow . . . won't you Rab?

When Krissie found Billy on the night of the opening, he was shivering in a similar way to that day in C hall, but for different reasons. He was coming off the junk and his folks had placed him under house arrest.

'Yeah, Chas came this morning,' said Billy. 'I'm sorry I did that to you, Krissie. See what this shite does? That's me, never again.'

He took a drag of his cigarette.

'What did he do? Where did he go? Was he okay?'

'He just asked me and I told him.'

'What did you tell him?'

'About Jeremy, that it was him.'

'What do you mean?'

'Got me to take the photos, and that horrible thing at Robbie's nursery – sorry, the guy uses every little bit of information you give him, be careful Krissie, what else did you tell him? He said he'd kill me if I didn't and he said he'd give me a daft amount of money. By the way, the gear in those fag packets, it was just washing powder.'

'Jesus Christ. But why?'

'He wanted to see if you would do him a favour.'

FIFTY-FIVE

After visiting Billy that afternoon, Chas's first thought was to make Krissie safe. He had to protect her. He needed to get to her straight away.

She wasn't answering her phone as he drove with one hand towards their flat. He parked and ran to the front door. As he reached the top floor, he noticed the storm doors were open. He stepped inside the small vestibule and something banged into the back of his head, something from the darkness inside the vestibule, and it hurt so much that it was almost a relief to lose consciousness.

Jeremy had a vague idea of what he wanted to do. It would be creative, as always, and symbolic. After making sure there were no neighbours about, Jeremy waited for his bait to arrive. He knocked him out, and pushed the floppy man up through the manhole in the close. He then pulled himself up into the attic, and landed on the unconscious body. Taking a few breaths, he gathered his composure, and then the materials he'd needed to make it work.

The attic was about twenty square metres, with an apex of seven feet. One side of the sloping wall had been covered in makeshift white plasterboard. An old coat was hanging on a large hook at the top. On the floor was a fake Christmas tree, some insulation, some old bits of wood, washing line and a large box of tools. Perfect.

Jeremy lifted Chas's limp body and secured the neck of his designer jacket on the hook that was bolted right through to the wood behind the plasterboard. It ripped a little, so he relieved some of the weight by placing a piece of wood between his legs and bolting it to the beam at one end. He tided his hands together in front of him with some of the clothes line, wringing his wrists with the last knot.

Chas woke with a jolt and kicked his legs into Jeremy's stomach.

'Well, hello,' Jeremy said, gathering his wind. 'You must be Chas.'

Chas kicked his legs out again and then yelled. He was wriggling on the white plasterboard like a spider about to be washed down the drain. His toes were inches from the ground. Eventually, he calmed himself with several shaky breaths, realising he'd have to do some fast talking, improvise.

'Krissie told me she loves you. She told me this afternoon,' Chas said. 'There's no need for all this. She's yours. Hasn't she tried to find you to tell you? She said she was going to go to you. If you let me down I'll give you her mobile number, and you can go to her.'

'Krissie told me you were clever . . .' said Jeremy. He then pounced from the floor so suddenly that Chas didn't have time to react. Jeremy pounded Chas's head with his fist.

'But I don't think you are,' Jeremy said to Chas's drooping head, as he tied his feet to the beam on the floor.

When Chas woke everything was dark. There was a moment of unawareness, a warm waking yawn, but it didn't last long, because he tried to open his eyes and he couldn't.

'You're as pretty as a picture,' came Jeremy's voice, which was very close to him but somehow separate.

Chas realised he'd been blindfolded with one of the prickly branches of the fake Christmas tree. He tried to move his hands, but over twenty lengths of super-strength clothes line had been strung around him – from neck to toe – and then secured to the wood surrounding the plasterboard. Chas wriggled and cried a cloth-covered cry. He was going to die.

Jeremy perused his work, smiled, and wrote 'Portrait of an artist as a dead man' on the bottom right of the plasterboard. He was very pleased with his creation.

'If you think you can keep her from me with those painter's hands of yours, you're wrong,' he said, smiling.

Chas felt a cold jagged metal against one of his hands in front of him. Then, to his horror, he heard the engine of the cordless jigsaw groaning into action.

FIFTY-SIX

He'd tended towards nice once, Jeremy. When he was two he'd cuddled his mum and she said he was her best boy and he said she was his best girl and nothing could ever tear them apart. When he was three she made him mashed potato with sausages and tomato ketchup and he said thanks, best girl, and she smiled back at her boy. And when he was four, he tried to help that time with Bella, he was kind of good then too. Just trying to help.

It was after that he became not so nice. After his father left him. After his mother stopped loving him, unable to touch or look at him, unwilling to discipline or support him. Year by year he became a little bit less nice, one time so angry that Katie his kitty ended up buried to the neck behind the tennis court and then mowed. Later there was the girl in second-year literature who chose Flaubert over him. And the time his Thai cookery teacher got a new favourite – Russell, who made great curry puffs, before and after he died. It didn't happen often, because he avoided love and cocooned himself in success: hiring, firing, driving the profits higher, successful busy important property. Then he met Amanda, and it seemed to start all over again.

Amanda, who was his, completely. Offered herself to him, alone, four hundred miles from grasp, and while his feelings for her were nothing compared to his love for his mother – indeed no one had ever come close – she was his, and he was hers.

He was hers after his mother disappeared out the back exit of the hospital, so desperate to not see him that she actually ran as she hailed a taxi. He was hers when he drove through the suburbs, on the motorway, through Glasgow, along Loch Lomond, Loch Long, Loch Fyne and the canal. Hers as he parked the car outside their honeymoon lodge, as he crept towards the front door with flowers and bubbly, and hers as he heard a noise inside that made him stop.

He looked through the window, and then dropped the lilies on the ground.

He waited all night by that window and watched as two women undressed and made love. He'd seen it many times before, wanked to it in real time and in memory, but this was not good. He was not part of this. This was betrayal. He'd been betrayed many times before, most of all by his mother. He began to feel the anger that he some-times felt. He breathed with it and fed it with constant watching. He watched them curl and cry and cuddle. He watched Amanda wake and get dressed and drive her hire car away.

Then he entered the honeymoon lodge, walked quietly into the bedroom and said, 'You must be Bridget.'

She covered herself up.

He moved in towards her, smiling.

She tried to get off the bed.

He stabbed her in the stomach.

She screamed.

He stabbed her in the stomach.

She cried.

He tied her up.

She whimpered.

He cut her carefully.

She dribbled.

He ripped.

She fainted.
He cut.
She bled.
He ripped he stabbed.
She died.

FIFTY-SEVEN

What would Chas do? Where would he go? He'd want to find the bastard and kill him, that's what, just as he'd done with Sarah's stepfather all those years ago. He was like that, Chas. Impulsive and a sorter.

I rang home and his mobile, but there was no answer. Where would Chas have gone next?

He'd have hunted high and low for Jeremy.

Perhaps Jeremy had discovered his mother had arrived to help him. Perhaps he'd gone there.

I phoned the police to tell them what had happened, but they didn't seem overly worried about it. They'd look into Jeremy's alleged behaviour in prison. But so what if my boyfriend had been missing for a few hours?

Angry and terrified, I drove to the Clyde View Apartments fifteen minutes after leaving Billy. Anne Bagshaw was waiting anxiously.

'Where is he?' she asked.

'I don't know. I couldn't give him a lift, in the end. I thought he might have come here himself.'

'No. He doesn't know I'm here. It was a surprise, remember?'

I decided not to tell her what I knew: that he'd been violent in prison, and had done everything he could do to get close to me. I didn't tell her I thought he might want to hurt my partner. If I did, she might help him get away.

'Can you let me know if he contacts you? Ring this number. He left something at the prison that he might want,' I lied.

'Of course,' Mrs Bagshaw said.

'Do you have any idea where he might have gone? He's ended it with Amanda. He seemed different somehow, Anne, seemed to have taken a shining to me for some reason. He knows I'm spoken for, although maybe I confused him – I was having troubles for a while – he was very embarrassed when I told him I'd never intended to make him think anything would ever . . .'

Anne seemed shocked, rightly so, I supposed. He'd fallen for his social worker and broken it off with Amanda.

'Oh God,' Anne said, slumping into a seat under the window, looking as though her mind was racing at a million miles an hour. 'If he's taken a shining to you, then perhaps he's looking for you. Perhaps he's gone to your house. Did you tell him where you lived, anything about yourself?'

She was right, of course. I had told him things about myself. Where I worked, about my flat in Gardner Street, and an image of the name on the buzzer flashed before me. He'd have found it, no problems, whether I'd told him or not. And what was he capable of, I wondered. Was he guilty of killing Bridget McGivern after all?

'One other thing, Krissie,' Mrs Bagshaw said as I turned to leave, looking up at me from her chair under the window. 'As soon as you see him, tell him I'm here. Tell him to come. First thing. Tell him I've prepared his favourite meal, as a celebration – mashed potatoes and sausages, with ketchup?'

God damn, it, I was so close to screaming at her. Fucking idiot. Your son is crazy and you've set the fucking table and mashed the fucking spuds?

'Will you? Tell him his best girl said so?'

That last bit sent a chill through me. All this stuff about best girls – it was clear she was as mad as he was. I had to get out of there.

'Of course,' I said. 'And likewise, if you see him first. Ring me on this number.'

FIFTY-EIGHT

Father Moscardini had been sitting in the same position, stiff and unable to move, since Jeremy had thanked him for his time. He was in the little wooden confessional inside the large chapel that looked like an ordinary chapel on the inside, but like a prison on the out. He'd been so pleased when Jeremy finally came to him. After weeks of talking their way towards it, he finally came, just before he was released. This would be a good day, the Chaplain had thought to himself, when a poor soul forgives himself for a terrible childhood accident and finds peace, at last.

He'd been sitting in that very spot, ready for the handing out of absolution and inner peace, when Jeremy began.

'Father forgive me for I have sinned. It has been a lifetime since my last confession and these are my sins. I started a fire, when I was eight. It was in the school basement and I'm really sorry.'

Father Moscardini smiled from his box, absolution was on its way; then Jeremy continued.

'I have killed seven . . . eight animals. Various ways, various breeds.

'I have raped one man and two women, hang on, no that's it, that is right, one bloke and two chicks.

'I have killed four people and tonight I'm going to kill a fifth and I hope, father, that you can forgive me in advance for tonight, a few more Hail Mary's perhaps?

'The first was Bella, but you know all about that, and that's another thing I was wondering about. If limbo's been abolished, is it backdated? Does she get her time waiting back, because she wasn't baptised, see, not yet? Just wondering.

'The second was a swat whose books won over me.

'. . . Then that little cook boy, Russell, who went well with lemon grass.

'Do you think it's normal for a woman to sleep with her mother? It wasn't pretty, a mother writhing while her daughter licked her nipple. Jesus, it made me ill to the stomach.

'So there you go, father, for these and for the sin I am to commit tonight I am so very sorry, and would like to thank you for reassuring me about the vow of silence the other day . . .

'. . . and for your time.'

FIFTY-NINE

Oh God, where is he? I'm at Gardner Street. It's dark inside. A few ricocheted street lights but otherwise dark and the wooden floor is black with lack of light. I walk down the hall and into the kitchen and see a blackboard and a sink but there's no one there. I walk into the living room and there are sofas and a television but there's no one there. I walk into the bathroom, Robbie's room, the hall cupboard. There's no one there.

I walk slowly towards our bedroom and I open the door and jump because what looks like a ghost is my wedding dress, hanging from the door. I take a breath and turn on the light, and see a beautiful rose on a hair clip resting on the chest of drawers. There's no one on or under the bed or behind the wardrobe and I turn to leave and see my dress again, in the light this time. It's covered in blood. I stand holding it, stunned, and a drip falls onto my forehead. I look up and see that blood is dripping from the ceiling.

I run into the close and see that the manhole to the loft is not closed properly. Mrs McTay is arriving home with her shopping and watches as I grab the broom from the kitchen, run back and yank it open. I haul myself up and into the attic. I feel around in the darkness and listen.

He jumps out at me with the yell of a monster, and pins me down on the loose boards.

I will never hurt you, he says, still pinning me, my girl. I will never hurt you.

But he will. He'll hurt anyone who dares to betray him.

Looking in his wild eyes, I now know he killed Bridget McGivern.

I'm lying face up and I see a painting. It's beautiful. Black liquid pours from it onto the canvas and floor. Oh God, it's Chas. His eyes are closed, his head's down, and blood is dripping from where his fingers have been sliced clean with the jigsaw that's buzzing behind me.

I scream when I see them on the floor, five little piggies in a deep black puddle.

Now that Jeremy's pinned me down he doesn't seem to know what to do next. He's looking at me, like a baby would, into my eyes, searching inside of me and I look up at my Chas, his eyes closed and dead, and I suddenly find what I need to find. I remember what Chas has said to me over and over again, about not looking properly at what's before me, about things not always being quite as they seem.

'Your mum's here. She's cooked mashed potato and hamburgers with ketchup.'

'What?' Jeremy says.

'Your best girl, she's here, she came all the way to get you, and she's waiting for you, at the Clyde View Apartments, top of Clyde Street, number 12.'

'Hamburgers?' he asks.

'Sausages, I mean sausages.'

'She's here? Really?'

'Yes,' I say. 'And she gave the alibi that got you out.'

'She did? Even though . . .'

'Even though it was a lie. Go to her, Jeremy. She's waiting for you.'

He loosens his grasp and I feel the wet of Chas trickling towards me and I am crying because my life is melting in that loft and I can do nothing about it.

He loosens his grasp, and his look moves away from my eyes to something elsewhere, and he stands up like some

228

alien who's been called back to the ship, and wanders slowly out of the puddle, down the hole, down the stairs, out.

'AMBULANCE! AMBULANCE! MRS McTAY! RING 999!' I scream.

I jump to my feet and go to Chas. He's supposed to be at the opening, but instead I'm holding onto his body and yelling for help. He's still. No movement. I untie his legs and I gently slap his face but he doesn't respond. I try to pull the wire from the wall but it won't budge. I take my T-shirt off and hold it on his fingerless stump, meaty and red, and watch the loft fill with thick hot blood. I bang my foot on the floor and yell.

I can't un-gag him, take his blindfold off, or even check if he's alive. I know what I have to do is hold hard onto his spurting stump.

It feels like hours before Mrs McTay finally appears through the manhole. 'Ring 999, Run! And get some ice!' I yell.

She doesn't ask why, she knows, because as she bends her head down to exit, she is confronted with five fingers that are not attached to anything. She screams. She suppresses the instinct to vomit, disappears, and moments later she's back with a bag, frozen peas and a frozen leg of lamb.

'Wrap them up!' I say as I hold Chas's chop, which spews between my fingers. And she does, she bags fingers with peas and lamb, and we hold bits of Chas and pray in that dark loft until the siren comes.

SIXTY

Jeremy sits at the dinner table in Clyde View Apartments opposite Anne, looking at his mashed potato and sausages with ketchup, and he can't take a bite.

'Take some,' his mum says. For the first time in years, she's sober.

But Jeremy can't take a bite. It's been too long in the waiting and he's not sure he can leave the waiting, so he takes a sip of his wine instead. His mum doesn't seem to mind waiting till he's ready, and eventually he is. He eats fast.

'It would have been Bella's birthday today,' Anne says, looking into Jeremy's eyes just as he realises. She holds his hands tighter to stop him fighting, to help him not fight, and he doesn't have it in him anyway, he feels so bad and so weak.

She couldn't leave him in prison. She'd known that since he phoned and said he'd been speaking to this social worker: 'This best girl, and I know what to do, even from in here I can sort it out.' She knew that even inside he was too destroyed to do anything but destroy. Knew his forehead gashes and neck-bruisings were like those he'd inflicted at holiday camp when he'd wanted to come home, smashed his head again and again against the rocks on the back beach, and he did come home, she had to take him home. Knew that Bridget was like his poor dog, Bobby, who she had walked and cuddled too much. Knew he'd destroy like he did the boathouse in Cornwell, the baby in Oxford, the breasts in

Crinan, whose owner he then cut from ear to ear, and stabbed twenty-three times.

And she knew that he would keep on finding a replacement to devour and protect with blood and that the next one he'd chosen was Krissie Donald.

Anne sits at that table in the Clyde View Apartments in Clyde Street and watches Jeremy's shocked face, and then his uncomfortable face, and then his rather desperate face, reaching, begging, gasping for life. It takes a long time, and she doesn't take her eyes away from him because she took her eyes away from him once before and she will never do that again.

He looks at her mostly, but sometimes at nothing when he thinks this might be the last time he can make that effort to get it in, get it in, get the air in with harrowing noise and no thrashing because he doesn't have it in him. He's too weak and he feels really really sick, Mummy.

Anne holds both his hands gently now. Her son's eyes soften and Anne can see, for the first time in twenty-four years, the eyes that made her cry with joy when they opened for the first time in the labour suite, the eyes that used to transfix her as they gazed up from her breast, the eyes that had gleamed high on the baby swing, that she had wiped bubble-bath from with a soft yellow flannel.

'I forgive you and I'm coming with you,' Anne whispers.

A tear makes its way down Jeremy's cheek. He smiles at his mum, then sinks head first into the mashed potato.

Anne strokes her boy's soft hair and then calls the police.

'There are two people dead at number 12 Clyde View Apartments, Clyde Street, Glasgow,' she says. 'Jeremy Bagshaw . . . and Anne Bagshaw.'

She hangs up and looks at the boy she brought home to the flat in Tower Bridge, introducing him to his room and his panda and his tiny cute baby-grow thingy. She kisses him on the head, then takes a large, laborious mouthful of the potato that frames Jeremy's head. She chews and you can see that it's hard to swallow but she manages, seven times, her fork scraping the fluffy spud that has oozed from the edges of her beloved boy's face.

She rests with her son around that table, their hands linked once more, ready now to say Happy Birthday Bella.

Happy Birthday.

SIXTY-ONE

When the paramedics prise Chas's hands free and remove his blindfold, I'm sure he's dead. His face is grey, not white, and he's still.

I pour tears onto him as we drive and I wail unhelpfully as the ambulance roars towards the hospital and I can't hear what the paramedic is saying.

He's something, stop shouting, you need to calm down, shut up. Have I just been slapped . . . 'HE'S ALIVE FOR GODSSAKE!'

I hear that bit, finally, and my grief shuts down momentarily. Can I allow it to? Can he be okay, my painter man, who has pictured me in every beautiful thing he's ever seen?

I float alongside his trolley, then wait for hours in a brightly lit corridor room, where other families also wait, some not for long because they've been given good news, others longer because they haven't, and if they leave it will be real.

What news will they deliver to me? Will he die here, my Chas?

I think of love stories, the circle of meeting and falling again and again. Would I never meet Chas and fall in love with him again? Walking towards him in my dry-cleaned wedding dress? Smiling when he renders my gadgets redundant? Looking up as he cuts the cord of our little girl, perhaps? Making up after he's bought a motorbike and decided our friends are all boring?

It's three in the morning when a doctor comes towards me

with a face that makes me jump to my feet and scream. 'He's OKAY!'

'He's okay. It'll take a while, but he'll be okay.'

I jump, we all do, hardly noticing the straggler from the last sad group watching us, wishing, and then finally leaving into the dark empty night.

I'm sitting beside him a moment later. His hand has been saved by peas and lamb, a dinner we won't be having for some time.

I hold his face in my hands and put my cheek to his.

'I love you!' I say into his warm sleeping ears. He mumbles something that I don't hear.

'What darlin'?' I ask.

'Is everything going to be okay?' he asks, just as I used to, sometimes in the middle of the night.

'Yes, baby boy,' I reply. 'Everything is perfect because you're going to be okay and I love you more than anything in the world.'

'More than pizza?' he asks.

I hesitate, then smile.

'There's something I need to tell you . . .'